THE SAFETY FIRST MURDERS

Drug addiction is growing more menacing both in Britain and in America. Drugs are being popularized in songs, on records and in plays. This is a fictional story, but based in part on fact, of the underground drug traffic in Britain. A death in a club, put down at first as suicide but later declared as murder, leads Manson, chief of Scotland Yard's Forensic Laboratory, into a strange story of drug dealings and death.

E. & M. A. RADFORD

THE
SAFETY FIRST
MURDERS

Complete and Unabridged

LINFORD
Leicester

First published in Great Britain in 1968 by
Robert Hale Limited
London

First Linford Edition
published 2001
by arrangement with
Robert Hale Limited
London

British Library CIP Data

Radford, Edwin, *1891 –1973*
  The safety first murders.—Large print ed.—
Linford mystery library
  1. Detective and mystery stories
  2. Large type books
  I. Title II. Radford, M. A. (Mona Augusta)
  823.9′14 [F]

ISBN 0–7089–4586–4

Published by
F. A. Thorpe (Publishing)
Anstey, Leicestershire

Set by Words & Graphics Ltd.
Anstey, Leicestershire
Printed and bound in Great Britain by
T. J. International Ltd., Padstow, Cornwall

This book is printed on acid-free paper

1

A telephone shrilled startlingly in a darkened bedroom of a mansion in Berkeley Square, that London caravanserai of the wealthy and exclusive.

It was six o'clock in the morning. Outside, the dawn chorus of birds had dissolved into silence; morning in the bowl of night had flung the stone that puts the stars to flight; and the false dawn had relapsed, momentarily, into pearly greyness in the sky.

The telephone which had momentarily ceased shrilled again. Doctor Harry Manson started uneasily beneath the bed sheets. Then, suddenly, he was wide awake. With a glance at the twin bed in which his wife was still sleeping, he reached out to the bedside table, felt the instrument in the darkness, and lifted the receiver.

'Yes?' he asked quietly.

'Manson?' the answering voice asked.

'Yes.'

'Fellowes here. Say, I'm sorry to disturb you at this hour, but I thought you would like to know — '

'Then don't keep me in suspense, Fellowes. What is it?'

'Barstowe is dead.'

For a moment there was silence. Doctor Manson took the instrument from his ear, and gaped at it. It was the odd unconscious gesture of shock. Then putting his ear to it again, he spoke softly into the mouthpiece. 'Barstowe . . . dead! How? When did it happen? He was all right when I left him last night. What was it? An accident?'

'He shot himself, Manson.'

'He . . . shot . . . himself?' Incredulity raised his voice two pitches in tone. 'How? . . . Where are you speaking from?'

'The club.'

'The club! Do you mean that he shot himself there?'

'That's right.'

'Incredible. What time was this?'

'About four o'clock as I make it. After you left they played bridge. He was dummy in the last game and a waiter called him to the telephone. He was away about two minutes, then returned and asked the waiter if there was a bed available, as he wanted to stay the night. He and I had a drink, and I went upstairs about three o'clock.'

'Who found him shot?'

'A whole pack of men. Parker, Macay, Scholes, Wanamaker and Ashurst. They were in a session of poker. You know their kind of session. Parker had just shovelled up about twenty pounds on a 'see you' and was dealing out new hands when they say they heard a loud bang . . .

'The night porter seems not to have heard anything. He wouldn't, of course, down in the hall, but the poker room being on the second floor as you know, and by the staircase to the bedrooms, it sounded very distinctly. The five jumped in alarm — I'm telling you as Parker and Wanamaker described it to me — and Parker dropped the pack of cards. Macay said 'that was a revolver shot and it came from upstairs!'

'They tore up the staircase, all five of

them, and the smell of cordite halted them outside Barstowe's room — or rather outside a room. They didn't know Barstowe was in it. When they got no reply to their knocking they burst open the door . . . Barstowe was slumped half in and half out of a chair, and quite dead.'

'You weren't with them?'

'Lord, no. I sleep on the other side of the club, facing the street. Actually, I'd been asleep. First I knew of it was a clatter of feet going past my door, and someone yelling for the porter. It awakened me and I peered into the corridor to see what the heck was going on. I thought the poker crowd were having one of their rough and tumbles, and I was ready to tell them to get to hell out of the corridors. Wanamaker told me what they had heard and I went along to see, told the porter to call the police, and then stood by the door until their arrival.'

'You did quite right, Fellowes. Who is there for the police?'

'A sergeant and a constable came round from West End. I don't know who they are.' There was a hiatus for a few seconds. Then, 'I say, Manson, what the hell happened to Barstowe do you suppose?'

'I can't surmise, Fellowes. I'll have to see the report of the police officers . . . Thanks for telling me.' He replaced the phone. Alice Manson stirred in the adjoining bed. Before her marriage, she had been Alice Mendover, only child and heiress of the millionaire financier, and had now been the wife of the Scotland Yard Commander for several years. On their marriage, the Doctor had forsaken his Whitehall Court bachelor flat for the Mendover mansion, in order that his wife might still be with her father whose home she had managed since the death of her mother. She had heard her husband talking on the telephone, but half-asleep without any appreciation of what he had been saying.

'Who was that, Harry, at this hour?' she asked. 'What time is it, by the way?'

'A quarter past six, darling. It was Fellowes.' He hesitated. Then slowly, and with hesitation he said: 'Barstowe shot himself in the club early this morning.'

She shot up in bed, and her hands went to her mouth. 'Freddie Barstowe? . . . Oh, no.' Shock held her for a space. Then came the inevitable question: 'But why, Harry? Why? I would have thought he was the last person in the world to do a thing like that.'

'I should have thought so, too, darling. But I don't know until I get hold of more details.'

Alice Manson slipped out of the sheets. 'I'll make a cup of tea, darling. Phyliss won't be up for an hour.' She busied herself with a tea-maker in the dressing-room.

★ ★ ★

The Assistant Commissioner (Crime) of Scotland Yard (Sir Edward Allen) wandered from his room in the Yard, up the staircase, ignoring the lift, to the top floor and into the laboratory of his forensic expert. He sat down in an armchair, a little breathless. 'Heard about Barstowe, I suppose, Harry?' Doctor Manson nodded. 'Fellowes rang me at six this morning. I've a skeleton report here from West End.' He lifted two sheets of buff-coloured paper. The A.C. and he were intimate friends; had been since, years earlier, Sir Edward had invited Manson, then as now a scientist and then a dilettante in criminology, to found a forensic laboratory and scientific department on the top floor of the then Scotland Yard with the idea of the police being able to dispense with the hitherto necessary practice of seeking outside experts in investigations, particularly homicide. They were Edward and Harry when together, and it was Sir Edward who had introduced his god-child, Alice Mendover, to the scientist one night in the Sporting Club of Monte Carlo — a chance meeting with her during investigations into the deaths of a Yorkshire family on the French Riviera; and he had been best man at their wedding.

'Damned if I can understand it,' Sir Edward now said. 'He seemed level-headed, prosperous and carefree.'

'I understand it even less, Edward. I was with him last night up to ten o'clock.

We were playing bridge in the club.'

'Good heavens! Was he normal?'

'Perfectly. In good form, as a matter of fact.'

'Noticeably so? . . . Forced exuberance, perhaps. It's frequently a sign of mental disturbance, you know.'

'No. He was his perfect natural self.'

'Incredible. Do you think we should do anything about it?'

'We have to, Edward. You know that.'

Doctor Manson was referring to the rule ordained by the A.C. when the Doctor became the homicide chief at the Yard, that any unnatural death of any kind in the Metropolitan area should be passed to Manson for investigation. This had followed the chance investigations of three cases of seemingly natural death which were proved by the doctor to have been secret homicide. The regulation applied also to suicides. A forensic examination had therefore to be made on Barstowe. He now nodded thoughtfully. 'I'll drop round and see Inspector Makepeace at West End, and call in the club to see what I can glean.' He slipped into an overcoat and walked down the stairs with the A.C., and out on to the Embankment . . .

. . . and into the strangest web of crime that Scotland Yard had ever been pitted against; an unholy alliance; ghostly in its mystery; fatal in its operations.

2

Inspector Makepeace thumbed through papers on his desk and lifted out an envelope. Opening it, he extracted a piece of paper and passed it over. 'The doctor's report, Commander,' he said. 'It arrived only ten minutes ago. Mr. Barstowe was shot through the heart, and death, he says, would have been instantaneous.'

Doctor Manson looked up. 'Through the heart?'

'That's right. For details . . . Sergeant McIver and a constable answered the police call at (he consulted a report) at 4.50. They telephoned me from the club and I went over. He was quite dead, of course. He seemed to have used the gun whilst sitting down and was half in and half out of the chair. The door had been locked and had been broken open by the charges of two of the club members. I suppose you already know that?'

Manson nodded. 'What was the gun?'

'A French automatic, 6.35 mm., that would be .250 in the English calibre.'

'Licensed?'

'No, Commander. It was lying a couple of feet from the chair. Apparently it had dropped from his hand and had bounced on hitting the floor.'

'Any note or communication left behind?'

'Nothing on the dressing-table other than money, a cigarette case and various small objects taken from his pockets before retiring. They were in a small heap.'

'His clothes?'

'Wearing them.'

'You mean he had not undressed?'

'That's right.'

'Where is the body now?'

'Where and how we found it.'

'Still in the club?'

'Yes, according to the A.C.s Standing Order — waiting for you to examine it.'

'Of course. Use your phone?'

'It's yours.'

Doctor Manson made five calls. The conversations, brief, were identical in words except for a surname. 'Will you come along to the club right away? I'll see you there.' Then, with the inspector and a sergeant, he went to the club.

The Dilettantes' Club is a three-storey Regency building in Covent Garden. Its members are, as its name implies, wanderers among the Arts and Sciences. The membership is limited and strictly vetted. It includes a famous surgeon, a leading mathematician, scientists in Doctor Manson and Fellowes, a logician in Wanamaker, a financial wizard in Macay, and Scholes a politician. Barstowe, the dead man, had been high up in the Foreign Office but had retired some years earlier.

There is in the club a comfortable lounge, an elegant dining-room, a well-stocked library and a billiard room on the first floor; card rooms, a television room together with a waiting-room on the second floor; and bedrooms on the third. It was up the staircase from the second floor that Manson, the inspector and the sergeant proceeded.

Bedroom number six was at the end of

a short corridor and looked out at the rear of the building. Its door with the lock splintered and pushed off from the inside by the force the men had used to gain admittance, had been pulled close and sealed by the police. Inspector Makepeace examined and then broke the seal, and Doctor Manson entered.

He stood for a moment just inside the doorway and let his gaze wander round. Though closely carpeted, the room was simply furnished with a single bedstead, an oak dressing-table, an armchair and a plain hard-backed chair. An oak wardrobe stood against one wall and a bedside table included a commode. There was a washbowl. Barstowe's body lay on the bed covered with a sheet.

'Everything is as we found it except that the body was carried to the bed to enable the doctor to examine it,' the inspector intimated. 'The chair was not disturbed and the revolver — you see where it fell.'

Manson nodded, and stared at the weapon which was small enough to be held in a hand without the muzzle showing. His eyes, deepset in their sockets, became almost slits, and creases gathered in the corners of his eyes. He stood without movement for seconds and then said: 'Can you show me, Inspector, just how was the body in the chair before it was moved?'

'I think so, Commander, but we have photographs taken at the time. What do you think, Sergeant?'

Sergeant McIver took a seat in the chair. He wriggled for a moment or two. 'I think this was the position, sir, as nearly as I can get it. Inspector?'

'Yes, I think so.'

'Thank you, Sergeant,' Manson said, moved across to the bed and turned down the sheet. Switching on the bed light hanging down from the ceiling he bent over the body. After a few moments he took a lens from a waistcoat pocket and passed it slowly over the area of the jacket covering the shot wound. Finally, he lifted both hands of the dead man, and inspected them.

The sergeant caught the eye of his

inspector. 'Lot of palaver over a suicide,' he whispered.

'Possibly, but the Commander is like that,' was the reply. 'Dead bodies are his business, though — ' He left the sentence unfinished as the Doctor bent down and slipped a pencil into the barrel of the revolver which he lifted, put it in a cellophane envelope and in the case he had brought with him.

Crossing the room to the window he ran his lens over the lower sash and inspected the woodwork. He repeated the operation with the inside of the doorway and the light switch inside the door. The inspector, smiling a little at this Sherlock Holmes-like peering, coloured in confusion as Manson turned unexpectedly.

'Quite,' Manson said with a grin. 'I know; but you remember the advice given by the Delphic Oracle to Polycrates hunting about at Plataea for the treasure of Mardonius?'

'Leave no stone unturned, Commander.'

'It's a good oracle for policemen, too.'

'Did he find it, sir?' the sergeant asked,

15

interestedly. He had never heard of Delphis or Apollo's Temple.

'He did, Sergeant. Deeply hidden as Mardonius had supposed . . . I've finished here . . . Oh, just a moment.' He looked over the dressing-table, frowned, and then covered with his gaze the floor of the room. 'Are these — ' he indicated the articles on the table ' — all that were found in Barstowe's pockets?'

'All except the wallet which we have at the police station for safe keeping.'

'You are sure of that?'

'Absolutely.'

'Odd. Then where is the key?'

'Key, Commander?'

'The doorkey. I gather the door was smashed to get to the man.'

'We've seen nothing of a key.'

Docton Manson inspected the door. 'There is no bolt,' he said. 'So the door must have been locked. Perhaps one of the members picked up the key.'

'Must have done, sir,' agreed the inspector with a touch of wariness in his voice; he frowned at a tantalising thought that came into his head.

3

Six Dilettantes awaited Manson in the club lounge. Each had put on a black tie as a mark of respect for their dead associate. Scholes, the politician, voiced their feelings: 'This is an appalling business, Manson,' he said. 'Is there any possible explanation of why he did it?'

'If you mean by that did he leave a note — no, not here. We haven't been over his rooms yet. There are one or two questions I want to ask you. I was with him myself until late last night. Fellowes here played bridge with him.'

'That's so,' Fellowes agreed. 'When bridge broke up these chaps' — indicating the company present — 'started up with poker.'

'How was he then?'

'His usual self — joking in a mild way.'

'What time was the telephone call to him?'

'I should say about 2.30, certainly not later.'

'You, Macay, had a drink with him after

17

that. Did he appear in any way disturbed with the phone call?'

'On the contrary, I thought he seemed cock-a-hoop about it. He called the steward and asked whether there was a room vacant, as he wanted to stay the night.'

'He didn't mention who had called him?'

'No.'

Manson frowned. 'You see,' he said, 'the riddle I am up against is this: Barstowe had been here since just before nine o'clock. And it wasn't until 2.30 in the morning, and after the phone call, that he thought of sleeping here. Why the late decision? Had it anything to do with his death? Any of you know when he went upstairs?'

Wanamaker said: 'I put it as somewhere after three. He watched us playing poker for some time.'

'Now, you heard the shot and rushed upstairs. The door was locked?'

'That's correct. We busted the lock with charges, right off. It was a bit rickety, anyway.'

'Yes, I've seen it. Who picked up the key?'

'Key?' The remark came from five throats. They glanced inquiringly at each other. Macay answered: 'We never saw any key. Somebody kicked the lock out of the way as we rushed in. We were too worried about Barstowe to worry about anything else. Why?'

'Nothing. Only it doesn't seem to be in the room, or on Barstowe, and the police haven't found it. You are sure the door was locked?'

'We tried the door after knocking. It wouldn't open, which is why we busted it open.'

'There wasn't a chair hitched behind the door because it wouldn't lock?'

'No. The only chair I remember apart from the one Barstowe was in was across the room. Candidly, Manson, when I go into a strange bedroom in a strange place I lock the door and leave the key in the lock, or put it on the dressing-table.'

'So do I. Barstowe's pockets had been emptied on the dressing-table. We examined all the articles, and the broken lock.

There was no key.'

The night porter, fetched from his home, said he had heard nothing of the happenings from his cubby hole by the front door. 'You were on duty all the time?' Manson asked.

'Never left except for a few moments when I nipped down to the kitchen to make a cup of tea, sir. That would be some time around four o'clock.'

'There were no callers at the club?'

'No strangers, sir. Only one or two members who dropped in inquiring if there were any messages.'

'That telephone call for Mr. Barstowe: did you recognise the caller — by his voice, I mean?'

'No — I don't think so.'

'Did he ask whether Barstowe was in the club at that hour?'

'No, sir. He said to ask Mr. Barstowe to come to the phone.'

'You told Mr. Barstowe he could have room six?'

'I took him up, sir, to make sure that the room was ready for occupation.'

'Had he any nightclothes?'

'Not that I saw.'

'You didn't hear any of the phone conversation?'

'No, sir. The box is soundproof, as you know.'

Inspector Makepeace, who had left the room, reappeared carrying an article. 'I've just checked, Commander,' he announced. 'The bedroom door was definitely locked.' He displayed the lock. 'The bolt you see, is extended.' His face wore a puzzled look.

Manson said: 'That is all we can do for the present. Thank you all for coming.' He turned to the inspector. 'You can remove the body to the mortuary, now. But I would like Chief Detective Inspector Kenway to be present when you do so.'

'You'll want a post mortem, Commander?'

'I'll do it myself with the Divisional Surgeon, if you will let me know the time convenient to him. Oh, and Inspector, have a search of the ground under that bedroom window, will you?'

'What do we look for?'

'I don't know. Nothing in particular. Anything you can pick up, and I mean anything. And you might seal that room again. I may want to go over it more at leisure. There are odd circumstances about this suicide.'

'Right, Commander. I'll do it myself.' He stared in perplexity at the Doctor's back disappearing through the lounge door.

'Crumbs, Inspector, what a carry-on over a chap shooting himself,' the sergeant said. 'Because it's a fashionable club and the chap is a nob, I expect. D'ye reckon he'd be on a lark like this if it'd been one of the lower classes who'd done hisself in?'

The Inspector eyed his subordinate reflectively. 'Yes, Sergeant,' he said. 'I reckon he would — that one.'

★   ★   ★

The Assistant Commissioner telephoned the Commander in his laboratory. 'Any explanation of Barstowe's conduct, Harry?'

'None at all, Edward. There are things I don't understand. Perhaps there are things in his room. I'm going there now.'

4

He changed his mind about the time of the visit. Partly because he wanted to appraise certain conclusions at which he had tentatively arrived from his observations and questioning of the club members, but principally because Inspector Makepeace had telephoned that the surgeon was free to join in the post mortem at once.

The Doctor was agnostically inclined in the matter of sudden death; apparent explanations or theories of the *raison d'être* held no standing in his mind unless they were proved, or could be proved, by material *facts*; he was always prepared to consider them as theorems and dismissed or demonstrably proved. Not until then would he attach the Euclid Q.E.D. He thought in the case of Barstowe that he had the conclusive proof he needed; he had little doubt about it; but doubt, however small, was a dangerous thing, and the post mortem might remove it.

In the mortuary Dr. Kinderdine was waiting for Manson and Merry (the Deputy Scientist) and the three of them, masked and robed, bent over the body. 'I want the jacket and shirt,' Manson announced. They were removed and placed by Merry in a cellophane bag and in a case he had brought with him.

The body was then stripped.

'Shot himself through the heart, they tell me,' Kinderdine remarked. 'And you want to know if there is any internal reason, eh?' He guffawed. 'Thinking of cancer, or something?'

Manson made no comment. Kinderdine opened the body. 'Well, through the heart is all right anyway . . . umph . . . small circular entry wound.' He turned the body over 'Exit wound much larger.' He probed the wound. 'Laceration of tissue through deflection of the bullet in the body. You *did* say he committed suicide, Commander?'

'You are the surgeon, Kinderdine.'

'Cagey as ever, eh? . . . No blackening round the perforation . . . no dark zone or hardened skin that I can see . . . '

'Try a lens on it.'

Kinderdine did so. 'No, none,' he said.

'Right. He's all yours now. See if there are any complications inside and let me know.'

Back in the laboratory, Merry examined through a powerful lens the dinner jacket and shirt spread out on a test bench. There were, he saw, no signs of burning and little evidence of powder marks. 'Pretty certain the gun was fired from outside the flame zone,' he said to himself. 'And that means at a distance in excess of two inches, the flame zone limit . . . We've no tattooing round the wound which puts the shooting target between a foot and three feet away.'

He whistled, and presented his notes to Manson when the Doctor appeared. 'Check, Doctor?' he asked.

'Not necessary, Jim. I know enough. I only wanted confirmation. Where is the gun?' Merry produced it from the cellophane envelope. There were no markings on it visible to the naked eye, but on fine chalk powder being blown on it from a sufflator and surplus powder being removed with a fine camel hair brush several fingerprints came into view. In the laboratory photographic dark rooms Wilkins, the laboratory chief assistant photographed the prints and enlarged from the negative. Comparison was then made with the photographs and specimens of prints taken from the dead man's fingers.

They showed the prints on the gun — the only prints — were identical with the fingers of Barstowe himself, up to sixteen points of resemblance.

The doctor and Merry stared at them, and at each other. 'Bit of a shock this,' Merry said. 'The other evidence is different.' Manson said: 'Send the gun and the prints to Fingerprints and ask for a report urgently.'

He went into his study and passed in memory over the conclusions he had reached so far in investigation. He pondered for half an hour. Then he spoke his thoughts aloud, which by itself was a measure of his consternation; there was usually nothing indecisive in his temperament. 'No, it's impossible,' he muttered. 'I *must* be right.'

Half an hour later he was with the A.C. 'Any progress, Harry?' Sir Edward asked.

'So far as I am concerned, Edward — yes. So far as certain evidence is concerned — no.' He opened the wallet he had brought with him and produced a photograph measuring ten by eight inches. 'This,' he said, 'is a photograph taken by the West End station people of the position of Barstowe as he was found in that room. Look at it.'

The A.C. gazed earnestly at the reproduction. 'Well?' he asked.

'See anything out of line in it?'

'No, I don't think so, apart from why Barstowe should have done it.'

'How would you describe the scene as shown?'

'As Barstowe slumped in his chair, obviously dead, half in and half out but held by the arms and the back of the chair.'

'Go on.'

'An automatic a foot or so away to his right.'

'Right. Inspector Makepeace takes the view that the gun dropped from his hand to the carpet and then bounced a little from the recoil.'

'Seems a reasonable assumption,' the A.C. admitted.

'So! How long had you known Barstowe?'

'I don't really know, several years anyway.'

Manson pointed again to the photograph; and Sir Edward scrutinised it again with intensity, laboured intensity. 'No,' he said.

Manson leaned over the desk, his face thrust forward. 'Why should Barstowe who was left-handed in everything — writing, holding a book to read, eating and gesticulating — *why should he shoot himself with a gun held in his right hand?*'

'Lord sakes!' ejaculated the A.C. and started up in his chair. 'You mean . . . '

'It was the first thing I saw when I entered that room and looked at the *mise en scene*. The dressing-table was the next thing; everything he had taken from his pockets had been placed left centre on the table. Now look at something else. The absence of a suicide note we will let pass; it may be in his rooms, though I doubt it. When he went to his bedroom at 3.30 he apparently locked the door. It had to be burst open by the men who ran upstairs. The lock bolt we found was extended. *But we found no trace of the key which locked it — and nobody remembers picking up or seeing a key.*

'Until 2.30 Barstowe had no intention of spending the night in the club; he had no nightclothes, no shaving tackle, not even a hairbrush. Not until he received a telephone message at 2.30 did he ask for a room. Why? Up to then he had exhibited no signs of concern or disturbance which are the concomitants of suicidal intention.'

'There is more?' the A.C. queried.

'Yes, the autopsy examination. When a revolver is fired in close contact with a body, as in a suicide, the jacket or shirt shows burning of the cloth from the flame which shoots out of the muzzle. We call it the Flame Zone. In the case of Barstowe there is no such burning.

'The entry wound when a gun is held close to a body is cruciform or stellate in shape with lacerated edges, and the exit wound is smaller in size than the entry. In Barstowe the exit wound was larger than the entry. There was no burning and no blackening on the jacket. Both Barstowe's hands were clean. I doubt whether you or anyone else could fire an automatic without leaving powder blackening on the hand holding the gun. I can try a paraffin test on Barstowe's hand, but it would be negative. You can be sure of that.'

'Well, Harry, the evidence seems conclusive. Where is, then, your trouble?'

'Here! *The only fingerprints on the gun are Barstowe's* — none others, and there were no signs of wiping previously.'

5

Paul Valèry wrote of Leonardo da Vinci: 'The folly of mistaking a paradox for discovery, a metaphor for a proof, a *torrent of verbiage for a spring of capital truth, and oneself for an oracle is inborn.*'

Doctor Manson was unaccustomed to mistaking proofs in investigation, and had not found himself out in one since the case of the deaths in the Château Noir at Menton, on the French Riviera. Nor had he been known to lapse into verbiage over a capital truth, until this moment of verbiage with the A.C. He was soon to acknowledge with a rueful smile his mistake — in fact within the space of a few minutes of settling down again in his study alongside the laboratory.

His telephone buzzed.

'Yes?' he answered.

'Commander . . . ? Francis speaking from Prints. Those dabs you sent for comparison.'

'Yes.'

'They are identical in every detail up to sixteen points of similarity. And that is cast iron, as you know.'

'True, Francis. One in 65,000,000,000 chances of being wrong.'

'Identical in *every detail*, Doctor.' He emphasised the two words.

'So you said.'

Francis withdrew the receiver from his mouth and stared at it, puzzled. The Doctor, he thought, could usually take a hint; a nod was as good as a wink to a blind horse. He listened again at the phone. Manson had by now felt a pricking suspicion in his mind at Francis's repetition of the phrase.

'What do you mean by that?' he asked.

'The actual prints of Mr. Barstowe you sent with the photographs of those found on the gun. Did you take them off Mr. Barstowe's fingers after death?'

'Of course.'

'Well, sir, so were the prints on the gun — rolled, I mean.'

'Great heavens . . . I see what you mean. Thank you Francis. I am very much obliged to you, especially for your thoroughness. Oh, by the way, do you know which hand was rolled on the gun?'

'From the position of the fingers, Commander, in relation to the gun barrel, it was the right hand.'

Manson carried the news to Sir Edward.

'*You mean, Harry that after Barstowe was shot someone pressed his fingers round the gun stock?*'

'And then dropped the gun, yes. Only the presser did not know that Barstowe was left-handed and he pressed the right hand. Why I didn't realise what Francis told me I'll never know. It was an obvious check to make. Everything else was in apple-pie order — the wound, the absence of burning, and so on, I must have been half-witted.'

'Well, Harry, Homer frequently nods, even in Scotland Yard you know.' (In actual fact the A.C. was just a little pleased to find that the infallible had for once proved fallible.) 'So it is murder, is it?'

'Undoubtedly.'

'By a member of the club? Oh, no!'

'That's what it looks like at the moment, unless we can find the presence of a stranger.'

★ ★ ★

Murder!

That meant investigation by the Homicide Squad and its Three Musketeers, as they were called in the Yard. The three were Doctor Manson himself (the Forensic head), Detective Chief Superintendent Jones, and Detective Chief Inspector Kenway; plus the aid of any of the C.I.D. staff to be called upon.

Jones, affectionately known to all ranks down from the Commissioner to detective constable as Old Fat Man (he weighed eighteen stones, waddled when he walked, and had a corporation which he said was muscle, and everybody else said was fat) heard the news along with Kenway from the Doctor himself. He asked for full details and was given the story of the night's happenings in a club.

For a moment he appeared to have

been stricken dumb. Then came the expected deluge — expected because it would be a carbon copy of numerous outbursts in similar circumstances. 'Cor stone the ruddy crows,' he roared (he always roared). 'You've bin at it agen. Pokin' and pryin', seein' ruddy murder in every flaming happenin' . . . you . . . you.'

It was Old Fat Man's idiosyncrasy to believe that Doctor Manson went out *looking* for murder in every case of death that came suddenly to anyone. Just for the fun of the hunt. In point of fact, he was pretty well right; the Doctor had an *idée fixe* that a percentage of deaths certified by doctors as from natural causes, and even a higher percentage by coroners as suicide, have been, and still are secret homicides, due to loopholes in the law. Accordingly, he probed every suicide brought to his notice (and natural deaths where he had the opportunity where unexpected demise occurred). In a number of cases he had, indeed, found murder.

He had, with pointed finger, emphasised the Dilettante Club death to the

A.C. 'Do you suppose, Edward,' he had asked, 'that if Barstowe's death had gone to a coroner's court there would have been any other verdict than suicide — on the apparent evidence?'

'No.' the A.C. had agreed.

The *idée fixe* did not, however, pacify Jones. 'Dammit, Kenny,' he said (turning to Kenway). 'Look at it. There's a ruddy cadaver in a club. Gone to bed all sudden-like without any nightclothes ... dead after a shot is heard behind a locked door ... dead in a chair ... a gun by his side and a hole in his heart, a nice cosy suicide, and he (pointing at the Doctor) has to go shouting ruddy murder. Now, we gotta go to work, me, trudgin' about in me state of health ... '

'It will get your weight down,' Manson said grinning. 'And some of that fat off.'

'It ain't fat.'

'Looks like fat to me,' Kenway said, and poked a finger in the stomach.

'Keep your ruddy hands off. Want to rupture me, or something. Pokin' like that.'

It was all the old fat man's blah-blah.

He was the oldest and best detective in the Yard, the most skilled and enthusiastic hunter in homicide, and Doctor Manson's most fervent admirer; and the Yard knew it and loved his pseudo 'paddys.' He came back to normal.

'This club charnel house, where is it and what is it?' he asked.

'The Dilettantes,' Kenway said.

'Has it been ribbed and . . . ' He broke off suddenly. 'Wot club did you say, Kenny?'

'Dilettantes.' A grin started to split the inspector's face.

'The Dilettantes! That's his own club. HIS club. Stone the flaming crows, he's goin' round startin' flamin' murder now . . . I reckon he did it himself to start us off detectin'. I'll lay a pound to a penny he was in the club last night — '

Doctor Manson opened his wallet and took a pound note from it. 'I was,' he said.

'You was?' Jones's face was a study. The Doctor and Kenway subsided into chairs and rocked with laughter. 'You'll be the death of us one of these days, Old Fat

Man,' the Doctor said.

'Ah . . . Ah . . . ' Jones said. 'You been too clever a dick this time,' and a grin illumined his face. 'You was there. You'll have your flamin' dabs taken and I'll see they're put on the file . . . Where do we start?' It was Jones the hunter uttering the last words.

6

Men of the Yard descended in a flock on the outraged, and indignant home of the Dilettantes. They puffed powder of different colours over the furniture and effects in the bedroom, and photographed all the fingerprints that turned up. They fingerprinted the staff ('for comparison and dismissal, gentlemen,' the operators explained). Later, laboratory attendants with a forensic vacuum cleaner swept dust up from the carpet for classification of the dust in a search for any outside, foreign, dust; and did the same with carpeting in the card room.

Outside, Kenway and Jones roamed the haunts Barstowe was known to visit, restaurants, amusements, card clubs, seeking from acquaintances any circumstances which could have engendered an intention or threat against his person; and to canvass friends, especially female friends, to whom he might have confided anything that troubled him, and in which he foresaw danger to himself.

Frederick Barstowe was in life a man to whom the term nondescript might with justification have been applied. An inch or so over medium height, he had brown hair, light blue eyes which robbed his face of any personality, and a sallow complexion. He was around sixty years of age and dressed always neatly, a fact which was negatived by a somewhat slouching gait when he walked, and which seemed to throw his clothes into some disorder. Coming down from Oxford after Eton at the age of twenty-five with a degree in political history (First-class honours) he went into the Foreign Office, and there he remained until, some two years earlier, he had unaccountably retired, much against the advice, and to the annoyance of that Department: for he had the complete confidence of the Minister and staff, mostly because of his knowledge of the politics of foreign countries, embassies and affairs of state. For years he had spent most of his time travelling in Europe and the Near East on confidential missions. He spoke seven languages.

His *pied à terre* was the ground floor of a house in Storey's Gate, a flat he had chosen for its proximity to the Foreign Office, Downing Street and Parliament. It was there that Doctor Manson and his personal secretary, Detective Sergeant Barratt, went in search of anything that might throw light on why anyone should want to get rid of a seemingly harmless man living in retirement.

The flat consisted of a large lounge and a smaller room adjoining, obviously used as a library and study, three walls being covered with bookcases, the contents of which were works on politics, covering the histories of countries, their development and financial and economic conditions. Other books were devoted to literature and classics — the library in fact of a savant. The flat had two bedrooms, a boxroom, a kitchen with a small gas stove and a few articles of cookery ware, together with crockery. A small passage from the kitchen led to a side door opening into a narrow alleyway which led into Storey's Gate. The furniture throughout was good but old-fashioned. Barstowe had apparently bought it when he started his career, and it had lasted him comfortably and satisfactorily. It was obviously a bachelor's flat; those little touches which reveal a woman's hand being completely missing.

The library seeming to be the more likely place for any discoveries of interest, the two detectives turned first to a large desk. It stood across a corner of the room where light from the window would fall over the right shoulder (Barstowe wrote with his left hand). Though not a rolltop, it had a row of drawers extending over the desk proper and drawers down each side of the leg aperture. In an opposite corner of the room stood a steel filing cabinet six feet high with six deep compartments. All the drawers of the cabinet were locked. The Doctor, with keys taken from Barstowe, opened them up, carried the contents to the desk and with Barratt began to examine them.

The contents consisted of stiff folders in alphabetical order and each inscribed with a description in the top right-hand corner. Inside the folders, foolscap size, were papers, the majority marked 'Foreign Office Top Secret.' Carrying the folders to the desk he and Barratt went over them side by side. The contents startled the sergeant.

'Gosh, Doctor,' he said, 'what the hell is he doing with these? They're explosive.'

'But ancient history, Barratt, though they'd cause a furore if the contents got out generally. As to what he was doing with them — ' He treated the documents to closer examination and breathed a sigh of relief. 'Carbon copies of his own reports and conclusions on investigations here and abroad,' he said. 'As author of the reports I suppose he had the right to keep copies for reference. The originals of course are in the files of the Foreign Office, or in the Cabinet secretariat. Nevertheless, I think they should go to the Foreign Office and not into the hands of Barstowe's executors. We'll take them along with us later.'

'Do you think they have anything to do with his death?'

'They are here, aren't they, Barratt?'

'*These* are here, sir. But are some missing?' Doctor Manson's brows came together in a frown. 'The room was sealed.'

'Since, Doctor — after Barstowe's death. Suppose something was taken before his death, and revealed how much he knew, and that he was dangerous.'

'So! We'll get the Foreign Office to check all his assignment reports and see if they are all here. But he has been out of the Office for two years, you know.' He returned to the desk. 'Hunt round and see if you can find a couple of suitcases and put the contents of the files and of this desk in them. We'll go through them at our leisure at the Yard.'

Carrying the cases, they left the flat after re-sealing both doors and windows.

7

Barstowe had been a member of the Dilettantes' Club for ten years, having been elected on the proposal of Norman Charles, an authority on the human mind, seconded by Alexander Purcell the mathematician and supported by Montague Fellowes, a Doctor of Science, who had held a Chair at Oxford and at Harvard.

The *aegis* under which he had gained access was Literature, and he had specialised in International history and economics. He was never a popular member and not much of a mixer, but was in great demand as a bridge partner being within a fraction of world championship class. It was known that he held at the time a confidential position in the Foreign Office, but he never spoke of his work there.

It seemed impossible to the Doctor: (1) that there was anything in his Foreign

Office association to lead to murder, since his connection with it had long been severed; (2) that assuming the Foreign Office association had anything to do with his death that it should be, as it appeared, that a club member should have anything to do with it.

All the members were well known in the world of Art, Science and Literature, and were men of repute in the general public. None of them could be classed as a possible murderer. It was true that murderers seldom look like murderers, despite the ideas of Lombroso, but the thought of a Dilettante indulging in homicide was, the Doctor thought, revoltingly incredible — except for the fact that Barstowe *had* been killed in the club. Politics played no part in the Dilettantes — indeed arguments on political creeds were banned, and they had no foreign members, or members who might be unduly interested in anything that might be affected by Britain's foreign policies.

The Assistant Secretary of State looked up from his desk in the Foreign Office.

He had spent half an hour going through the carbon copies which Doctor Manson had carried from Storey's Gate. 'The Minister will be extremely obliged to you, Commander, for rescuing these documents from prying eyes,' he said. 'There are too many of these so-called Top Secrets springing up — out of motor-cars, left in trains, scattered over the countryside, and heaven knows where else.

'There is nothing of importance in these' — he tapped the files. 'The only Top Secret about them is the disclosure that we are showing interest and peering into things other countries are doing in certain directions. There is not, however, anything underground about them.'

'I wonder that men are allowed to retain carbon copies of state reports,' Manson said.

The Assistant Secretary laughed. 'An eye to the possible future, Doctor. Most of the personages in government service have always the idea that they may write publishable and revealing memoirs, or newspaper articles, you know. That's how autobiographies come into print. Reports such as these are 'proof tablets' so to speak, evidence of accuracy. Of course, they couldn't publish these without permission. But they could give the gist of the contents — and the Foreign Office would be in a cleft stick, unable to confirm or deny.'

'Why did Barstowe leave the Foreign Office?'

'I don't know. It was quite unexpected. He seemed always satisfied, and he sacrificed some pension by going when he did. I mean to say, few of us knew the Middle East and the Far East like he did. His leaving was a blow to us.'

'And to me,' the Doctor told the A.C. on his return to Scotland Yard. He found Kenway and Jones still sorting through the collection of papers, etc., brought from the flat. 'Nothing so far, Doctor,' Kenway reported. 'Letters by the score, accounts and so on. He seemed to hoard things like a squirrel. Little notes on various topics, even receipts for every derned little thing.' He waved a paper. 'Here's a receipted bill for a week's newspapers. Why in Hades name did he want to keep that? And here's a bill for fifteen and sixpence for a tie.'

'Ruddy wonder he, being what he was, didn't want the damned receipts in triplicate,' Jones said.

'Give me a bunch,' Doctor Manson said; and began a methodical search into the pile Kenway passed over. He went through and discarded a pile. 'Better see they go to the executors, Fat Man,' he ordered. 'We've no authority to retain them, and we don't want them, anyway . . . More please.'

Kenway passed over another selection in a parcel labelled, 'From bottom left-hand locked drawer.' It contained papers taken from that drawer of the desk. The Doctor tumbled the contents out on the table and began a search through them. There was nothing of seeming interest until he picked out an envelope of a cheap variety such as is contained in packets, with paper, sold in all shops in the City. An unformed and illiterate hand had written the address:

Mr. Aaronson
Upstairs,
No. 15 Water Street,
London, E.

Inside was a half-sheet of equally cheap and dirty paper. With puzzled interest Doctor Manson extracted it and read over its wording:

'To month's rent, £3' with underneath, the word

'Paid.'

The Doctor eyed it for a moment. It was, he thought, a curious document to be in the possession of Barstowe and, from the address, from a person obviously of inferior standing. He called across the room:

'Where is Water Street, Fat Man?'

'Water Street . . . Water Street?' Jones's brows drew wrinkles as he cogitated. 'Oh . . . ah . . . got it. Lumme, ain't come across that name for years — '

'Where is it?'

'Down Wapping . . . off the High Street. Why?'

'Come here.'

Old Fat Man waddled across. Manson handed him the envelope and contents. Jones read the message out. 'Who's Aaronson?' he asked. 'What's he got to do with Barstowe?'

'Looks like Barstowe's got property down there,' Kenway suggested.

'Come off it. This is a receipt TO Aaronson,' Jones said. 'How's Barstowe got hold of it? It's a rum area down there, Doctor.'

Manson looked at him, and he said: 'I'll go and have a look-see and a palava.'

'Take a car.'

'What! An' leave it while I takes a dekko in Water Street! Damn, we'd have it pinched in less than five minutes. Bus for me.'

8

The Fat Man went by bus, a tedious ride. He could have gone more easily by Underground to Wapping, but wanted, nostalgically, a view of the streets and corners of the area in which he had spent many days and nights (mostly nights) to the detriment of wrong-doers, who had breathed sighs of relief when his figure no longer appeared at awkward moments.

Chuckles came from him now and then as various passengers boarded the bus on its route, caught sight of the superintendent out of the corners of their eyes, decided they had made a mistake in the number of the bus, and hurriedly left. The superintendent had been the terror of the underworld for years, knew all the habitués by sight, and also knew their modus operandi.

One, a woman, was not quite quick enough. She boarded the bus half-way along the Commercial Road and took a seat beside the superintendent. Jones looked sideways at his seat companion. So did she — and rose. The superintendent, smiling genially, pulled her back by an arm. 'Well, stone the crows,' he said, 'if it ain't Whizzie Malone. An' goin' all the way to the docks.' He thought for a moment or two. 'Now what ship from furrin parts would be goin' to be paid off today,' he mused.

'Look, Mister Jones, it's nice seeing you again after so long a time, but you're making a mistake. You got me all wrong. I'm straight. I am, and I got to get off now. I'm meeting a man at the next stop.'

'If it's about a dog, ducky, you needn't worry. I gotta bit o' bad news for you. The poor wee beastie's dead and gorn. Died of distemper. Tell you what I'll do for old times' sake like. I'll get orf with you and put you on a bus goin' to the Battersea Dogs' Home.'

His baby face with its benevolent expression changed alarmingly to ferocity. 'An' if I hears from the dicks at Wapping as how some pore fellow 'as been whizzed, I'll have you in gaol before you've had time to say 'Hallo, sailor'.'

He carried out his self-imposed escort duty and waved the lady good-bye after her parting words: 'Bloody rotten dick.' Then, chuckling loudly, he caught the next bus travelling in the direction of his destination. For 'whizzing' is crook slang for a pickpocket and he had taken Whizzie Malone into East End courts a dozen or more times for picking up seamen, plying them with drink, and then whizzing their hard-earned 'paying-off' money at the end of a voyage. 'Must be fifty if she's a day — and still at it,' he said to himself.

Jones left the bus at the corner of Leman Street and Dock Street. He waddled his eighteen stone along The Highway, turned down Wapping Lane and off into Water Street, a thoroughfare having access to Wapping Basin and the main docks. Drab with age and dirty with rubbish blowing from gutter to gutter in the river breezes, it housed a public house, one or two shops and a few decrepit houses let out in rooms to seamen. Number 15 was an apology for a ship's chandler's establishment. The window, clouded with the unwashed dirt of years, could hardly be seen through, but contained a heterogeneous collection of articles — marlin spikes, ditty bags, pots and pans, compasses, oilskins, boots and shoes and heavy woollen socks all piled higgledy-piggledy together.

At the side of the shop were three steps up from the pavement leading to a door giving access to the residential part of the premises. A woman sat on the top step, the open door behind her; an old woman dressed in a grimy skirt and cardigan, and peeling potatoes into a bucket held between her knees. Grey hair pulled back to a bun in the nape of a dirty neck looked to have strained the skin of the face back with it, so that it resembled a wrinkled chamois cover stretched tight by her projecting nose. Jones approached her.

'I wonder if you can help me, Missus,' he said. 'I'm looking for a Mister Aaronson.'

'Don't know if he's here, Mister.'

'Oh, but he lives here, don't he?'

'Gotta room, if that's what you mean.'

'Well, ain't that livin' here? How long 'as he had the room?'

'Dunno fer sure. Months perhaps.'

'Pays the rent?'

'Ruddy well has to, else he'd be out, Mister.'

'When was he last here?'

'Dunno. I'm only the bloody skivvy fer the boss. Might be up there now fer all I knows. So long as he pays the rent that's all that matters. The lodgers comes and goes as they pleases.'

'An' you don't know whether Mister Aaronson is in, eh? Can I go up and see?'

'Please your ruddy self.'

Jones mounted the rickety stairs. Dirt lay everywhere. A smell of stale food permeated the entire atmosphere. Stair treads were loose; on the landings part of the floorboards had rotted away. Banisters had long since vanished. Old Fat Man wheezed and moaned as he lifted his eighteen stone upwards at the immediate peril that his weight might precipitate him through the worm-eaten boards. Aaronson's room was one of two on the top

56

storey. Knocking at the door produced no reply, but presented a surprise — the door swung open on a room empty of any occupant.

From the doorway the superintendent saw a scene of desolation — and more. A chair lay on its side near a table. It was smashed and had apparently been flung with considerable force. A second chair was leaning drunkenly against a wall. The remains of a meal lay on the table, with two battered tin mugs. The superintendent, advancing gingerly into the room, stopped and sniffed at the dregs in the mugs. An empty whisky bottle stood near them.

Moving over to the broken chair he pulled up at the sight of a stain on the dirty, uncovered floor. The floor was in fact marked with stains all over; but what had halted Jones was the nature of this particular stain. He knelt down and scrutinised it closely.

Leaving the room and descending he went into the chandler's shop. 'Know anything about a chappie named Aaronson?' he demanded.

'Tenant top floor,' the chandler said.

'When did you last see him?'

'Never seen him at all. Took the room off the old girl.'

'Bit odd, ain't it? You're the owner of the property.'

'Her looks after the house.'

'I want a hammer, a couple of good staples an' a padlock, cully,' he said. 'To lock up Aaronson's room. He ain't there an' I don't like what *is* there.'

'Why?' The superintendent showed his warrant card.

'Blast! What's he been doing?'

'He ain't bin doin' nothin' that I know of — yet. The point is whether anythin's bin done to him, son.'

Jones drove the staples into the door and lintel, padlocked them and pocketed the key. Then he wandered along to a police station and telephoned Doctor Manson.

'You think it's a bloodstain, Fat Man?' the Doctor asked.

'I don't think. I ruddy well know it is.'

9

Doctor Manson drove down to Water Street in a Yard 'Q' car which was, in fact, a taxicab with the engine hotted up; it wouldn't have been wise at any time to wander along the East End in a noticeable police car; there was likely to be a general exodus of people troubled by something on their consciences. Chief Inspector Merry was with him, together with a fingerprint operator and a photographer. Jones awaited their coming.

The Doctor surveyed the interior of the room from the doorway. 'Nothing has been touched,' the Fat Man said. 'It's just as I saw it. I only went up to the table and the stain.' He nudged Merry, 'What'yer think of it, son?'

The Deputy Scientist knelt down by the stain and peered. 'Almost certainly blood, Fat Man,' he agreed. With a scalpel taken from the murder bag he scraped a quantity of the stain and emptied the specimen into a plastic packet. It went into the bag. The cameraman went into action and when he was clear, the fingerprint man took over, searching various areas of the room through lenses and with insufflator and soft brushes and a variety of coloured powders. In fact all the panoply of homicide went into service, though there was no certainty that there had been any homicide.

'The glasses have been wiped, Doctor,' he announced, 'but there are a few smudges on the table edge, and on the door lintel, the latter left-hand prints by the way.' The prints revealed by the powder were photographed.

'The bottle?' Manson asked.

'Clean, sir. That let's me out. I'll go back and get the photographs developed and printed.'

'Send the prints to Records to report to me.'

With the retinue departed the Doctor and Jones began an examination minutely of the room. It is what is euphemistically called a bed-sitter and had a part at one end divided off with a plywood partition extending some three feet from the wall. The bed was an iron contraption with, on it, a filthy straw mattress, a stained bed and dirty army blankets. The area behind the partition contained a small, cracked wash basin and a cupboard, with in it a stale loaf of bread, a saucer in which were the dried remains of rancid butter, a half packet of tea and a bottle of wine. On a rickety wooden ledge extension to the washbasin was a small gas ring, a leaking kettle, dirty cups and a plate. A curious spicy aroma permeated the place.

'Rum do, ain't it, Doctor,' Jones said. He scratched his head in perplexity and met the Doctor's glance. 'Damn me, I don't think the fellow lived here at all. I'll lay five pounds to a penny nobody has slept on that ruddy bed for months. Lumme, it's like a piece of concrete. Only, mind you, the table's bin used, an' the glasses. What in hell do you suppose the chappie had the room for?'

'Curiouser and curiouser,' Manson said. He accepted the Fat Man's word. Jones knew more of humanity and life in the East End than he did — he had spent half his life in it.

The situation was to become even more curious. The Doctor, extending his area of search, bent over the bed and kicked against some hidden obstruction. Stooping down he felt under the bed and pulled out an aluminium ladder. Closed, it measured about four feet long; extended in its three parts, it stretched for eleven feet. The two gazed at it in perplexity. 'What, Fat Man, do you suppose is the purpose of this?' Manson asked.

'Escape in case of fire — out of the window.'

'What!' He crossed to the window opened it and looked out. 'An eleven foot ladder to get down there! There's a drop of over thirty feet.' His eyes wandered upwards, and stayed. Jones's eyes followed him. In the ceiling was a boarded aperture, three feet across. 'Now, what would be the object of that?' he quested. The Doctor was signally ignorant in the material things of life; there was with him an almost child-like questioning of points which are of everyday knowledge to most people. Jones enlightened him.

'Trapdoor, Doctor. Top storey this, under the loft. Water tanks are in the loft. Ladder to give access, I reckon. Got one like it at home. Have to have it. Water pipes up there, too. Go all round the eaves, round the outside walls. Never learn sense, our ruddy plumbers, You'd think they'd have the nous to put 'em along an inside wall to protect 'em from frost. Only they don't.'

'And you reckon that's the explanation?'

'Damn sure it is. If a tank freezes, and springs a leak, that's how you get to it, through the trapdoor.'

'Well, let's make sure, shall we?' Manson's dictum was never to take anything for granted. He was always more doubting than Doubting Thomas, and persisted in probing until, like the gondoliers of Gilbert and Sullivan, there remained no 'probable possible shadow of doubt, no shadow of doubt whatever.' He proceeded to make sure, extending the ladder and pushing one end on the aperture raised it on its hinges. With Jones holding on at the bottom in case of its slipping he began to climb up. Waist-high with the ceiling, he stopped.

'Good God!' he said; and hoisted himself into the loft. Jones yanked the bed over to steady the ladder and hauled himself up.

'Well, whaddyer know,' he said.

The loft extended over the width of the whole house, with a chimney stack rising through the centre. Two water tanks were at one end. A small window light in the roof of the building gave a little interior vision. But it was neither of these things that had elicited an expletive from both detectives.

The loft was furnished, after a fashion.

Amid all the dust, the cobwebs, the layers of dirt left by the years, there were rude furnishings. A folding table stood beneath the skylight, in front of it a folding chair of the kind popular at seaside resorts. An oil lamp stood on the table.

Across a corner were stacked several books on top of each other, Manson lifted them: Rowell's *Battle of the Wolves of Society*, Tuohy's *Inside Dope*, and Quincey's *Confessions of an English Opium Eater*. The last book opened itself at a page on which a paragraph had been underlined. The Doctor read it with a frown on his face:

Thou only givest these gifts to men; and thou hast the gifts of Paradise, O, just subtle and mighty opium.

He showed the passage to Jones who said 'What the hell!'

A cardboard box underneath the table contained cigarettes wrapped in paper. The Doctor put one to his nose and sniffed, then replaced the cigarettes in the paper and in the collection of things in his case. He picked up the cardboard box. 'There's quite a collection here. We'll go through it at the Yard.'

They clambered down the ladder into the room below. The Doctor reaching up from half-way down slid the trapdoor over the aperture saw it drop safely into place. The ladder he folded up and replaced under the bed. They left, repadlocking the door behind them, walked down the rickety stairs into the street. The squad car was round the corner.

10

'God bless my soul,' the Assistant Commissioner (Crime) said. He screwed the monocle into his perfectly good left eye. He stared through the window at the traffic on the river below. It had begun to move and a south-easterly wind was springing up, rustling the trees on the Embankment. 'Dear me, you think this man — what's his name, Aaronson — has been disposed of?'

'I don't know, Edward,' Doctor Manson said.

'There's evidence of it?'

'Only a very large and nasty bloodstain — human blood.'

'Could have been an accident, perhaps?'

'We've had every hospital in the area contacted. None of them knows Aaronson, or has had any wounded or injured person admitted.'

'Perhaps he did not need a hospital or treatment.'

'With the amount and nature of the blood revealed in the lab, he certainly did. We're having all doctors telephoned, just to make sure.'

'But, damn it all, Harry, I don't get it. What has Aaronson to do with Freddie Barstowe?'

'We found a receipt for a month's rent of the hovel in which Aaronson lived among Barstowe's papers in the Storey Gate flat. That's why we went down to Wapping.'

The monocle fell out of the A.C.s left eye, and tinkled against a waistcoat button. 'For God's sake, Harry, are you suggesting that Barstowe — '

'I'm not.' He denied the unspoken suggestion. 'We don't even know that Aaronson is dead. We don't know what has happened to him except that the old woman who looks after the building says she hasn't seen him for some days.'

'Who and what is Aaronson?'

'Again — we don't know. Haven't any idea. Wapping police know nothing of him — never heard his name. The local income tax people know nothing about him; he has never made any tax return. He has never been on the dole; there is no National Health Card in his name. No works in the place has employed him. So far as we can find he has bought no food from any of the shops in the neighbourhood, and the public houses have no knowledge of him as a drinker.'

'And what in heaven's name,' the A.C. asked, 'was he doing roosting up in a loft when he had a room down underneath?'

It was a point that had been exercising the mind of the Doctor himself. It was pretty evident from the conditions disclosed in the loft that Aaronson had spent a considerable time up there. The furnishings — if such a description could be applied to the table and chair — were better than those in the room below; the folding canvas chair was a more restful article than the hard-backed chair below, and the folding table was at least firm on its legs. Too, he had his books in the loft — strange books for someone living in the conditions of Water Street; ordinary denizens of the area were hardly likely to be reading *Battle of the Wolves of Society* or the *Confessions of an English Opium Eater*.

But why did he migrate to the loft at all? Why not have made the room below more comfortable, poverty stricken though it was? Why? . . . Privacy? For what? There was nothing in the room to suggest that he had anything of importance to conceal. And what thing of importance, anyway, would a man living in such circumstances possess?

Fear — of what? Until something was known of the man there could be no answer. It seemed to the Doctor, however, to provide a possible clue. Aaronson could climb into the loft, draw up the ladder and close the trapdoor and be secure from prying eyes. If for some reason — which it was impossible to conjecture at the moment — he feared attack at night, he was safe from any would-be assailant who would conclude that the expected occupant was out. There was, the Doctor thought, some support for this theory in the fact that the bed below had never been slept in; its condition showed that only too plainly.

He pushed speculation on this point aside for the time being for something of far greater moment — why he (the Doctor) had ever found himself in Wapping at all. He had started out to investigate the murder of Frederick Barstowe, a friend and a fellow member of the Dilettantes' Club; a man of brilliant position, of education and fastidious in his tastes; only to find himself in the course of his inquiries saddled with what looked like a second murder of a mysterious person, a down-and-out in a filthy hovel in the East End of London, a man who lived amidst destitution — a gulf as wide as that which separated the Rich Man from Lazarus lay between the two men. How come?

Coincidence? Doctor Manson did not believe in coincidence in cases of sudden death; he had stated so a hundred times and was wont to explode when the word was used in connection with incidents arising during investigations. What was called coincidence, he maintained, was an event materialising out of another event, and a natural consequence one from the other. Thus, the connection with the East End was a natural consequence of the finding among Barstowe's papers in the West End of the receipt for a month's rent of the East End hovel. It had obviously been given in to the Water Street address and had found its way to Storey Gate. *How had it come into the possession of the fastidious Mr. Barstowe?*

Was Barstowe responsible for the disappearance of Aaronson? It would seem that he must have visited Water Street in order to be in possession of the receipt.

'Then why?' Kenway asked, 'if he had rid himself of Aaronson for reasons we don't know, should he bring away a document like that of no use to him, but the very possession of which placed him in the room of the bloodstain, and could prove disastrous when found among his belongings?'

'Saw a play once,' Jones volunteered, 'Mikado . . . line in there I remember 'cos it tickled me, a dick.'

They looked at him for enlightenment;

it didn't seem to have any association with the matter in hand. 'Woman, nice looker, sang, 'Ah, make no mistake.' ' He chuckled. 'It's by their mistakes that we catch 'em. Like happened here — bringing away that receipt.'

Manson looked at him. 'You think that Barstowe — ?'

'Don't *you*, Doctor?' Jones asked.

11

Now, a week before this story began the bar of the Navigation Inn, which is in Wapping, was crowded with a cosmopolitan collection of thirsty customers. The landlord is a burly man known far and wide, on land and sea, as Sailor Birkeley. The cognomen was nostalgic rather than factual; Birkeley had been a sailor once, but not during the last twenty years. He was a popular landlord on the whole but inclined to be ultra strict for the East End on the conduct of his house and when, and if, trouble arose, or an argument became unruly, left his bar to eject the obstreperous customer — a job for which he was particularly wellfitted, and which he carried out very well.

On the particular night connected with this narrative the customers consisted of a few seamen, a lot of stevedores, dockers and transport workers from the dock railways. They included, also, a stranger who was better dressed than most. He was burly but in a pleasant, not brutal, way, better spoken than the average run of the Navigator's customers; in fact he was more than a little out of place in the company. His white hands did not appear ever to have been engaged in any manual labour. The dawning of a beard marred his face, or as much of it as could be plainly seen, for he wore a pair of dark glasses, suggesting that his eyesight was not all that it should have been.

A pint of bitter for which he called was pulled by the landlord himself. Being a pleasant personality and noticing that his customer made no attempt to mingle with the company, he engaged him in casual conversation. 'You a stranger round here, sir?' he suggested.

'Yes, landlord. Came down to look up a friend on the *Melbourne Maid* that docked yesterday, but he'd gone ashore or something.' He looked round the bar. 'You seem to have a good trade here, or is it a special night?'

'No, pretty usual. The best trade in this area this pub is. I've been here twenty years, so they know me and I know them.'

'I'd have thought it might have been a rough house, down here in the docks, supporting a couple of chuckersout, you know.'

'Lor' bless you, sir, no. They're mostly gentle as lambs. They knows what would happen to them if they started anything like that.' He looked round his drinkers. 'There's only two of them that wants watching — them over by the door there.' The stranger eyed the pair — heavily-built men in jackets and thick grey jerseys, and trousers tied above the knees with a thin strap, their faces coarse and hardened. Each was holding a half-pint tankard of beer.

'Dockers?' the stranger asked.

'Labourers, when they work at all which isn't often.'

'Ah, there's a lot of them about like that these days. They seem to get by somehow.'

'Dole drawing and public assistance does that, sir.'

'I dare say. You and I have to pay to provide them.'

It was a quarter of an hour later that the pair, their half pints finished, put down their tankards and left the public house. The stranger who had dallied with a second pint, looked at his watch, finished off his drink and also left with a 'good night' to the landlord.

Outside, the two men were walking along the narrow street. Quickening his pace the stranger caught up and walked alongside them.

'Like to cop fifty nicker, you two?' he asked.

They dropped to a halt and stared at him. 'For what?' The pair spoke as one. 'You was in the pub wasn't you?'

'I was looking for a couple of likely lads.'

'What? To give 'em fifty nicker? You ain't a philanthropist, I reckon.'

The stranger told them. 'Better drop in here, guv'nor,' they said, and slipped into an entry between two shops. In the shadow of the alley they argued for a few minutes. 'It's money for old rope,' the stranger insisted. 'The place is deserted at this time of night and the whole job won't take more than ten minutes, if you handle it right — like men taking a drunken pal home?'

'The doings now?' one of the pair said.

'Half now, balance when the job's done. I'll pay you on the spot.' Twenty-five pounds changed hands.

Out of it was to come a third murder.

And this time there wasn't any likelihood of it being coincidental.

12

'I don't know, Jones,' Doctor Manson had replied to the Fat Man's question on Barstowe — 'Don't you, Doctor?' In fact as was the case with the A.C., the point had been unpleasantly active in his mind; and the fact that the last time people in Water Street had seen Aaronson was some two or three days before Barstowe's death.

Kenway brought some relief to the situation for a moment. 'Look, Fat Man,' he said, 'if it was Barstowe, why was Barstowe himself killed?'

'A good question,' Manson said. 'He *was* killed, you know. Had it been suicide, I would have felt inclined to go along with you.'

Jones fiddled with his tie. His eyes looked past the Doctor and Kenway: looked, as it seemed, through the wall and down the river on its way to the sea. 'I know the East End, Doctor, better'n any dick or crook who lives there. They live hard down East, and they live by the law of survival. I reckon there's never a night in them parts when there ain't acts o' violence. Somebody starts an argument and there's a bloody punch-up. Somebody gets his head bashed about, or gets shivvied, bicycle-chained or stabbed or somethin'. An' what happens? His pals gang up on the bloke or blokes who hit or stabbed him and work on him. It don't matter a dime whether he had been in the right or wrong. One of their mob was knocked out, and they don't stand for that. There ain't individuals down there; there's mobs. They've only one law, an' it's a good Biblical law — eye for eye, tooth for tooth, hand for hand, foot for foot — '

'Exodus, Chapter 21,' Kenway put in, helpfully.

'If Barstowe outed Aaronson an' if they know'd it down there, then Barstowe had it coming to him. And you'll have a hell of a job to find out who did the coming, sure certain. They don't sing down there; they'll know nothing. It's happened times and again down East and we never clobbered anybody.'

'But in the club, Jones.'

'It don't matter if it were in heaven, Doctor.' He paused and looked back in memory. 'Now me, I know'd a man (when he was looking backwards and remembering, Jones was wont to lapse in grammar and syntax) who outed somebody. I know'd he done it, and every dick in the East End know'd he'd done it. We couldn't prove it though there were people as see'd it done, an' he was walking free as air until he died naturally. Then there was a girl murdered in a Bayswater basement. The Yard here know'd who'd killed her, only we couldn't prove it, couldn't even get enough evidence to arrest him. Laddies, the Yard tailed him for years. He knew it and laughed at us. He's still walkin' around today — or he was the last I heard of him. No, Doctor, if it was Barstowe, an' I ain't a sayin' it was — only suspicion — then Aaronson's buddies got their eye for an eye, even in a club.'

Doctor Manson eyed him sombrely.

There was little he could say in reply. Jones knew the East End like he knew the backs of his own hands; had spent a lifetime among its denizens. 'Well, we'd better go through this stuff from Water Street,' he said, 'and see if it provides anything.' He produced the cardboard box taken from the loft. It was about two feet square and two feet deep with a folding cover to contain its contents.

Wearing rubber gloves, the Doctor opened it up. 'Better get someone down from Prints, to be on the safe side,' he warned. As each article was lifted out of the box Prints scrutinised it after it had been laid on the table. With the box emptied the table presented an odd and unexpected appearance.

'Flaming Jupiter,' Jones roared. 'Was this 'ere Aaronson a skirt or a ruddy hermaphrodite?' There was some justification for the outburst; the table collection included a tin of grease, another of cleansing cream, a bottle of liquid for staining or colouring skin, eye-black, and eyelash brushes, a cake of soap and a half a dozen paper

82

towels. At the bottom of the box in a cellophane bag had been a wig of black, untidy hair. When fitted to a head it would have been long in the neck and curling upwards at the nape, and would have developed into sideburns below the ears. The result would have been something like the arty-crafty Beatle-type hair style.

In a smaller box were a teaspoon, with the handle bent at right angles, a piece of candle, and an envelope holding several tablets that looked like saccharine tablets. There were also an eye-dropper and a long needle stained dark-brown at the point. The stain could have been blood.

The Doctor surveyed the articles, and for once astonishment showed on his reserved and somewhat aloof face. 'And there are no prints on anything?' he asked.

'If there were they have been eliminated, Commander. There are prints on some cards, but so many and so overlaid that they are useless for identification purposes.'

'Ah, yes, the cards.' He fingered them.

They were pieces of printed pasteboard, membership passes for night clubs — one for the Inferno Club with a West End address, and another entitling its holder to pass into the Club Volante. It was the first ray of light in the investigation. The cards had been used and it was obvious that other members of the club must know something of Mr. Aaronson; he would have mixed with them. If there was any link between Barstowe and Aaronson the clue could lie in the clubs.

'Know anything about these places, Old Fat Man?' the Doctor asked. Jones shook his head. 'Must be recent. I've never heard of them.'

The Doctor dialled on the intercom the office of the Assistant Commissioner 'A' Division. It is the division of the Yard which deals with administration and general duties in the Yard, and the Doctor put the question to them. 'Oh, yes, we know them Commander,' Assistant Commissioner Philpot agreed. 'We've been watching the Inferno for some time, but there's nothing we can move in for, so far as we know. The Volante has mostly a foreign membership and has a French counterpart in Paris. Why? Anything wrong?'

'The man Aaronson had a membership card for both clubs. We're trying to find him — or his remains.'

'Want us to move?'

'No thanks, not at present. We'll try for something at this end.' He clipped up the intercom lever and looked with a smile at Jones. The superintendent shied away.

'Oh no! Oh no you don't,' Jones roared. 'I'm out'a that. Stone the crows, Doctor. I'm known in that manor. I'm the best known dick in London. If I as much as put a foot inside the door of that place being the place 'A' Division think it is, I'd empty it in a couple o' minutes. An' I'd stand a good chance of being laid out.'

Manson nodded appreciatively. 'You may be right, Fat Man. We'll have to think of something, though.'

13

There was to come almost at once a further pointer, and one which seemed likely to be of more immediate assistance. While the three were still debating the matter of the clubs, Chief Inspector Merry, the Deputy Scientist, looked in at the Homicide General Office. 'Are you wanting to know anything about prints brought in by a photographer, Doctor?' he asked. Manson looked up expectantly.

'Because if you are, Prints say that the dabs left on a table leg and on the door lintels in a place in Water Street are in Records under the names of William Moore and Nicholas Monrose. Any help?'

Jones let out a whoop. 'Slasher Moore and the Mick,' he roared. 'Cor stone the crows. They was in the Water Street hovel? That's a turn-up for the books.' He paused and thought deeply. 'Sure there ain't any mistake, son? Ain't like the Slasher to leave dabs behind.'

'No mistake according to Prints,' Merry insisted. 'You questioning it?'

'Know anything about them Fat Man?' the Doctor asked.

'Cor lumme, yes. Robbery with violence . . . served eighteen months and three years, that's Slasher . . . moniker 'cos he uses a flick knife. Nick the Mick has been inside half a dozen times. Snakes, though, wot in hell are they doin' in cohorts? They don't work together.'

'Well, their fingers are in Water Street,' Merry said. 'And over a bloodstained floor. And Slasher, you say, uses a knife.'

'Pull them in,' the Doctor ordered. 'Put out a general call.'

'I'll have a look round,' said Jones. 'I'll lay a pound to a penny as Slasher don't know he left dabs. Where'd they find his?'

Merry looked at the report from Prints. 'Half-way down the left side door lintel.'

'Humph! If he and the Mick were edging a weight through the opening, he could ha' stumbled and shoved out a hand to save himself — the heavy weight bein' Aaronson. That's damned bad luck, a thing like that 'appening.' He shook his head: it looked like a sorrowful gesture.

'Look,' Merry said, 'Whose ruddy side are you on, you fat bladder of lard.'

★ ★ ★

Doctor Manson wandered upstairs from the Homicide General Office to his study which adjoined the laboratory. It was a handsome room, furnished and carpeted beautifully, a fact which usually came as a shock to visiting police officers due there for conferences on deaths in their areas. Their reports back home that Yard men did themselves damned well was a little misleading; Doctor Manson was a wealthy man, a Doctor of Law as well as of Science and Medicine; and had been an amateur criminologist before the time that Sir Edward Allen, the Assistant Commissioner (Crime) had seduced him into entering the Yard.

Sitting at his Sheraton desk he reviewed in mind the situation in the light of the new developments. He felt in much better spirits than when he had left the study for the discussion with Jones, Merry and

Kenway; and lighter than had been the case half-way through those discussions. The identified fingerprints were responsible for the change.

There is no argument over fingerprints; if Records stated that the prints at Water Street were those of certain people — then, they were. Jones had knowledge of both men as being violent and having convictions for violence. If they had been present in that room, then Aaronson's disappearance was associated with them — and accordingly *not* with Barstowe.

He said so, with relief, to the A.C. when Sir Edward looked round the door, and seeing Manson, entered. He was puffing from the climb up a flight of stairs — the lift had not been extended to the top floor — and sat heavily in a chair. 'These damned stairs will be the death of me,' he moaned.

'Well, get it altered, Edward.'

'You go and talk to the Receiver about the expense.' (The Receiver is head of the Yard department dealing with finance and maintenance.) 'Any news?' he asked; and was told.

'Two men — they being the ones, I suppose, for whom a general call has gone out. Anything about Aaronson?'

The Doctor pointed to the table on which were displayed the articles taken from Water Street. 'There,' he said.

The A.C. walked across and eyed them. 'God bless my soul,' he ejaculated. (It was his usual expression of surprise.) 'What was he — a vaudeville artist . . . impersonator?'

Manson made no reply, but roamed round the table fingering various articles and setting them straight on the table. There was no reason for this; but he seemed to be composing his thoughts. Finally desisting, he answered the question: 'He was apparently a man who lived always in an atmosphere of fear.'

'How come, Harry?'

'He was, or is still, a man of light-coloured or little hair. So he wore at times a black wig and he disguised his personality by what is in effect a beatnik hairstyle.' He fitted the wig to his own head to demonstrate — 'as you see. Now, the contents of this bottle' — he indicated it — 'are to darken the skin. The eye-black and eyelash brushes are to darken what are light-coloured lashes and brows to match the hair colour; he had to disguise his appearance for somewhere, possibly to use the night clubs for which he had membership cards. The clubs, by the way, are dubious ones. 'A' Department have been watching them for some time without effect at present.'

The A.C. acknowledged the explanation. 'And the fear?' he asked.

'Disguise is obviously one pointer. One does not go around disguised unless there is some good reason why one should do. Then, he had a room but prepared a hide above it — in a loft. Now, let us arrive at a logical conclusion. He is sitting on this night in the room below as his usual self — bear in mind that the wig, etc., were in the loft above and not in use. Then that very thing against which he had taken precautions happened. He is surprised and attacked. The blood is evidence of that. And that is the last seen of him. It is all we would have known of him except for the fact that his attackers had no knowledge of the existence of the hideout in the loft. Any objection to that theorising?'

The A.C. fingered his monocle. 'No . . . sounds reasonable. And what are we doing about it?'

'We are looking for Moore and Monrose. They are the only people we know to have been in the room. The call is out, and Jones is scouting round.'

*　*　*

Jones *was*. He spent the afternoon wandering through old haunts but without finding traces of his quarry. He had, however, one piece of luck in a public house in Stepney. His entrance caused a sudden silence in the conversation, as he stood in the doorway. 'Evenin' gents,' he said jovially, and grinned. 'Don't stop 'avin' a natter 'cos o' me. An' nobody need hop it; I ain't nickin' anybody.' His glance round the room lighted on a couple of women, sitting at a table in a corner of the bar. He sauntered through a nervous company and up to one of them.

'Well, well, Ellen,' he said, 'long time no see.'

'Flaming Dick!' she said.

'Now, now, naughty. I've nuthin' agen you. You're a good girl now, I hear.' He looked down at the table. 'My . . . my! . . . double whiskies . . . Doin' yourselves proud, aren't you? Come into money?'

'Hop it,' Ellen said. 'I don't want to be seen talking to no dick. It ain't good for me reputation.'

'Lord, Ellen, it won't do you no harm talkin' ter me. I'm the nicest dick in town.' He called across to the bar; 'Alfie, bring the girls another whisky, an' I'll have one meself.' He waited for the barman to arrive, and raised his glass. 'Here's health — and luck, when you want it,' he said. The women drank grudgingly.

'Well now, how's The Mick these days?' he asked.

'Workin',' Ellen said.

'Look you now. Is he? I'm a bleeding prophet. I allus said as how he'd get tired of being in and out of the nick all the time. What's he doin'?'

'Building trade.'

'Building trade? Lumme he must be the foreman if his missus can run to double whiskies. Allus used ter be half a pint o' light ale. Where's he workin'?'

'Flats, Battersea, nosy.'

'Ah well, there's nuthin' like honest work.'

'No? You ought to try it, copper.'

'Copper . . . *Copper*? You insultin' me, Ellen? Dick is the word. An' me — honest work! You ought'a know better'n that. It's dishonest work as keeps me in whiskies.' He eyed the company listening interestingly and silently. At the door he turned. 'So long,' he said and eyed them balefully. 'Be seein' you, I *don't* hope.'

'What in hell did *he* want?' somebody asked. News of the call for the Slasher and Mick was known only to police officers at the moment.

At a Battersea building site Jones found the foreman. 'Superintendent, Scotland Yard,' he said, showing his warrant card. 'Got a laddie name of Monrose workin' for you?'

'Yes.'

'I'd like to have a word with him?'

'So would we. The bastard hasn't been near for days.'

'Lumme, come into money, has he?'

'Must have. There's two days' wages due to him. What's he been doing?'

'Nothing so far as we know. He may be able to tell us something. Suppose you haven't got a buddy named Moore as well?'

'We did have . . . sacked him . . . always fighting.'

'Yes, he would be. Pal of Monrose?'

'They was always drinking together.'

14

That was all Jones had to report when he trailed up to Doctor Manson's study and interrupted the discussion between him and the A.C. 'Not a sign of 'em,' he said. 'Ain't been around for days. But they got money. Monrose's moll is drinking double whiskies an' Slasher's upholstered and ain't been working for it.'

'You think they robbed Aaronson, Fat Man?' the A.C. queried.

'Search me. D'ye think Aaronson looked like a bloke who had money? If he had any and this couple outed him you can bet your life they pocketed it.' He turned towards the door. 'Be seein' you downstairs — about the club, Doctor.'

'You were saying when Jones blew in?' the A.C. said.

'Was I? About what?'

'Aaronson — more about him.'

'Oh yes.' He picked up the small case that had been inside the cardboard box, and opened it. 'Now here is a possible clue to the man's habits,' he said lifting out the candle, the tablets, medicine dropper and the teaspoon, and laying them out on the table. The A.C. bent over them, looked up and met the Doctor's gaze. 'What the devil are they for?'

'A drug addict's emergency outfit, Edward. There is only one item missing — a little rubber packing.' He picked up the teaspoon. Its handle was twisted so that it formed a right angle to the bowl. The inside of the bowl was stained. 'Now,' he said, 'this is only a suggestion.' He lighted the candle. Then he fitted the needle into the end of the dropper twisting round it a piece of cellophane tape to make a tight fitting.

Into the spoon he poured a few drops of water from a carafe and dropped one of the tablets into it. He then held the spoon over the lighted candle until the water began to steam and the tablet dissolved. 'It wants about half a minute for completion,' he said. 'Now I take the cap off the dropper, pour in the liquid from the spoon, replace the cap — and there you have it.'

'Have what?' the puzzled A.C. demanded.

'A shot of heroin. If you'd like to try the experiment? . . . no? Well, then, I'll explain it. You bare your arm, or your thigh, slip the needle under the skin for about half an inch, press the rubber bulb of the dropper — and you've had your shot.'

'Good God, you mean that Aaronson was an addict?'

'Until we find him I don't know. If he was then his arm will show the marks of punctures. You can't disguise them. If this is what he was using then I don't think Aaronson had much in the way of money to finance Moore and Monrose, or he would have provided himself with a hypodermic syringe. This way he risked poisoning.'

'The tablets are heroin?'

'Heroin caps, yes.'

'Well, that seems to settle that,' Sir Edward said. The Doctor remained silent. 'Doesn't it, Harry?' he asked plaintively.

'It could.' Manson hesitated, walked

back to his desk and sat down. Lines crossed his forehead and creases appeared in the corners of his eyes. It was a sign Yard men recognised: that he was troubled. The A.C. who knew the signs, waited.

'The snag I see in the apparent facts, Edward, is the presumed killing of Aaronson. People don't kill addicts; they encourage them. And I should doubt Aaronson had money enough, judging by his surroundings, to have become hooked on heroin.' They left the study together, the Doctor for the Homicide General Office; the A.C. to return to his own room.

There had been no results so far to the general call for the wanted men. Their usual haunts had been visited and their associates questioned. It appeared they had vanished from their surroundings some days before; the last anyone remembered of them was seeing them one night in the Navigation Inn. The woman Ellen, inquiries revealed, had been flush with money over that period and had spent what was, for her, freely.

She was kept under surveillance, but had not made any move in the direction of the men. The Yard's 'narks' and Jones's corps of informers alike had produced no clue to either of the men.

The matter of the clubs was brought up by Jones who still had a sneaking feeling that he was destined for the adventure. The Doctor reassured him. 'I think you are probably right, Old Fat Man,' he said. 'You'd possibly be identified — '

'Certainly, not possibly,' Jones said.

' — and you aren't the type for this kind of club.'

'Oh! An' why not?' The superintendent became obstreperous. Kenway laughed.

'Because you'd probably have the floor down in the cellars when you started to dance.'

'Dance?'

'Of course. Why the devil do you think night clubs are frequented?'

'No, I think on the whole Kenway had better go,' Manson said. 'He doesn't look like a detective, can mix with women and is presentable and hail-fellow-well-met with the male sex. I think, however, that he must look a little less prosperous.'

'Right,' said Kenway. 'How do I get in?'

Jones guffawed. 'Don't worry about that, son. Just walk in the door and say you want to join. The bloke on the door will have a peep at you, take a fiver and hand you a membership card. It ain't the Dilettantes, you know.'

Doctor Manson briefed him on the visit. 'You knew Aaronson only casually from a meeting and remembered his invitation to drop in when you found yourself at a loose end in London.'

15

Mrs. Alice Hedley went out for a walk. She lived in a house appropriately named 'Sea View,' at Saltdean, which is a suburb of Brighton, lying between that resort and Peacehaven on the climbing coastal road. After her evening meal she had cleared away and washed up, straightened the cushions in the lounge and had laid out the things for early morning tea. Her husband having gone for a drink — his usual habit — she decided that Rover, a black retriever dog who was squatted on the carpet wagging his tail hopefully, should have his late night walk.

It was turned dusk when they set out together. The end of their road joins Marine Drive, the coastal highway that runs, under various names, from Brighton to Peacehaven above an undercliff promenade. At Saltdean it also runs alongside a grassy bank extending for a considerable height above road level. It was along this bank, with the sea far down below it, that Alice and Rover went for their walk.

The verge has its ups and downs in hollows and mounds and between rather disconsolate clumps of bushes blown out of shape by the hard winds coming in from the sea. The hollows in summer nights are the sleeping resorts of tramps where they lie, covered with newspapers; and frequently not only during the summer months.

The walk had been in progress for some minutes when Mrs. Hedley became somewhat perturbed by the antics of Rover. He had been cavorting ahead and returning to her side with joyous barkings; but suddenly stood still some distance ahead yelping and refusing to return. He continued to bark, in spite of her calling, and in a higher pitch than usual.

Mystified and annoyed she went back to him. At her approach he withdrew a few steps and, turning, invited her to follow. She did so until he stopped at a bush. Looking down Mrs. Hedley saw a man prostrate in the grass. 'Good dog,

Rover,' she said and leaned over the figure. 'Are you ill?' she asked. There was no response. She bent down and touched one of his hands. It was icy cold. She turned him half over and felt his forehead. It, too, was cold. 'He's dead,' she said. 'Oh, my God, he's dead.' Half walking, half running she reached her home and telephoned the police.

Detective Chief Inspector Perry with a sergeant and constable were there within a quarter of an hour. Under the light of electric torches he knelt alongside the man. A minute or two later he was on his feet again. 'Sergeant, take the car,' he said. 'Get back to the station and bring a photographer. He'll want lights. Bring a tarpaulin and tent pegs and another constable. As fast as you can.'

'Right, sir. By the way the ambulance is below.'

'Tell them to wait.'

The photographer's lights and the ambulance excited the attention of road traffic. A line of cars pulled up in each direction, the occupants attempting to climb up the embankment. 'Constable, send this mob about their business,' the inspector ordered — 'and see they go. If they don't, take the numbers of their cars for an offence under the Road Traffic Act. Tell them they can't park by the roadside at night on this highway.' They can, he said to himself, but they won't know it.

With the photographer finished, the position of the body was marked on the grass, and the tarpaulin spread over the spot and pegged down. A constable was posted to keep away spectators until daylight allowed a more thorough examination of the spot to be made. The body went off in the ambulance.

A police surgeon, called from his bed, examined the body stripped of clothes. 'Stabbed six times,' he said, 'and any one of them could have been fatal.'

'Time of death, Doctor?'

'Impossible to say. You know that, Inspector. But at a rough estimate not less than forty-eight hours.'

'What! Dammit, he couldn't have laid there two days without being discovered.'

'That's up to you, Inspector. I said not less than forty-eight hours. It could be longer. On the average a body begins to stiffen around seven hours after death. In about twelve hours the body is rigid and stays that way for anything from thirty-six to forty-eight hours after death. This body is coming out of rigidity. Work the time out for yourself.'

The clothes, when searched, provided no clue to identity beyond a screwed-up piece of paper that had squeezed through a hole in a jacket pocket into the lining. It was a receipted bill from a London clothing store. In consequence, a report of the discovery, together with a description of the dead man, was telephoned to the Information Room at Scotland Yard with a request for any information they might be able to supply. The Information Room passed the inquiry on to the Homicide Department.

There, it came to the eyes of Superintendent Jones who had read it through three times before realisation came to him.

'Jumping crows in Hades,' he said. 'It's Slasher Moore. Bin done in. Blow me down, who'd do that to Slasher?' At this point his mind clicked backwards; he was a bit slow though sure in thought. He remembered back to the room in Water Street. 'Lumme, the Mick! What's happened to him, d'ye reckon?'

He jumped to the telephone. 'Get me Brighton C.I.D . . . pronto.' To the answering voice he demanded and got Chief Inspector Perry. 'That cadaver o' yours, Inspector. We identify him. He's a bloke handy with a knife we know as Slasher Moore — dangerous.'

'So? Well, he met a man even more handy with a knife and he's not dangerous any more, Superintendent — except perhaps, as a typhoid risk.'

'We've been lookin' for him — general call out.'

'What for?'

'Murder suspect. Now look — he had a mate name of Nick Monrose. We're lookin' for him, too. They were together. You have a good look round and see if you can find him, alive or dead.'

Jones rang off the long distance call, and phoned Doctor Manson. 'Sure it's he?' the Doctor asked.

'From the description — yes.'

'Then we'd better go down and make sure.'

In the mortuary Jones took one look at the body. 'Yes, that's 'im,' he said, and giggled. The Doctor looked at him in surprise. Jones coughed, apologetically. 'Sorry, I was thinkin' o' me old mother, God rest her soul,' he said. 'She was a pacifist all her life and had a war cry — '

'A what!'

' — I mean a peace cry. 'Those as live by the sword shall perish by the sword.' She'd have rejoiced at this 'ere corpse. Those as live by the knife shall perish by the knife. Lord knows, the Slasher lived by the knife — or the threat of it.'

As they walked back to the police station Jones muttered: 'Lumme, I wonder.'

'Wonder what?'

'I wuz thinkin'?'

'Well, think out loud.'

'There were two men in that room at Water Street. We reckon they outed Aaronson — right?'

Manson nodded. 'It looks that way,' he

said. He began to see inside the superintendent's mind.

'Then one could witness against the other. Now, one witness has been eliminated. You think that Monrose might have done the eliminating?'

'I dunno.' Jones scratched his head. 'The Mick ain't never been in violence — not till he got tied up with the Slasher. I'd ha' reckoned it would ha' been the Slasher who'd ha' done the eliminating — to out a witness.'

They drove with the inspector along the coast road. A constable drew out the tent pegs and pulled back the tarpaulin. The Doctor and Jones knelt down alongside the outlined body position. 'Did your doctor say how long he had been dead?' Manson asked.

'He said not less than forty-eight hours. There's something funny about that. This bank is a popular walk and even a sleeping man couldn't be overlooked over that time — '

'Nor can a surgeon overlook *rigor mortis*, Inspector. The body was limp, wasn't it? The man wasn't killed here.'

'No?'

'Not enough sang-u-in-any refuse,' Jones said. The inspector staggered a little. 'Not enough — what?' he asked.

'He means blood, Inspector,' Manson said. 'Don't mind his long words. The man was stabbed six times and obviously bled to death. There isn't a jugful of blood soaked into the ground here. I should say he was killed elsewhere — and heaven knows where that could have been — and his body brought here in a car and dumped You might try inquiries into boarding establishments of all kinds whether they booked two men into a room during the last few days. You've got the description of this one.'

Jones said: 'Or just this man or another singly. D'ye think they'd separate, Doctor, when they hooked it from London?'

'Not if one of them killed the other, Fat Man. You can't stab by remote control.'

16

Leaving the South Coast police to carry out the local inquiries the Yard men returned to London. Superintendent Jones, still searching for information which would provide clues to the identity, and the whereabouts of Aaronson, paid a visit again to the East End, making a round of the public houses.

It was on his fifth half-pint in the fourth public house visited that he felt a tap on his shoulder. A voice said: 'Cor blimey, you been put on observation duty again?' He turned quickly and: 'Gor'a'mighty, Ted Kelly. Well, wacher know. How long since we were last in a pub together?'

'Ten years.'

'That long? Made you a sergeant, didn't they?'

'Right — to bring up my pension.'

'Poppycock. You deserved it. Remember — '

'Look, Herbert, come round and see the missus. Always talking about you, she is. Says you've got on a bit since the old days and why didn't I get in the Yard. Me, I says, I never had brains of that kind.'

'It ain't brains, son. It's intuition I got, an' modus operandi. Know somethin'? I'm a bloody 'uman filing cabinet an' them people up there picks the cards out'a me brains.'

Edward Kelly had served all his police life in 'H' Division of the Metropolitan Police, which embraces among other areas, Leman Street, Limehouse, Poplar and Wapping. He had been a constable when Jones was a sergeant in the uniformed branch of the same divisional area. Arthritis had forced retirement on him and he had left some years earlier, and lived in a small house in Poplar.

Maria Kelly received the Fat Man with open arms. 'Fancy seeing you again, Herbert,' she greeted. 'I'll brew a cup of tea and we'll — '

'You ruddy well open a couple of bottles of beer, my girl,' Kelly exploded. 'Who the hell wants to drink tea at nine o'clock at night? I'm going to have a wash. You talk to Herbert — and open that beer.'

'Sit you back in that armchair, Herbert,' Mrs. Kelly ordered. 'How's Emma?'

'The missus? Oh, she's fine. Gettin' a bit fat you know, like me.'

'Aye, you've put a bit on I must say.' (Yard men would have been dumbfounded not to hear Jones put out his impassioned plea that it wasn't fat, but muscle from too much walking after wrongdoers.) All he said was: 'You gotta nice comfy place here, Maria.'

'It's not too bad. Ted's pension isn't what it might be but he's got a retainer from Securit as a guard. They calls him out two or three times a week. It helps. You going to retire?'

'Me! Not likely. Mind you, if I don't get me deserts — '

Kelly came back and Maria went out to prepare a supper snack. The two men went on a journey down Memory Lane. 'Do you remember . . . ' 'remember . . . ' It was Kelly who at last asked the obvious question. 'What in hell are you doing wandering round these parts again, Herbert? Reckon you aren't homesick for the old days, not after all this time.'

'No. Damme. They wuz all right at that time. You remember The Slasher?'

'Moore? Of course.'

'He's dead. Knifed at Brighton.'

'Lawks. You don't say. What for?'

'That's it. It's a damned funny story.' Jones told it at length, from the scene in the Dilettantes' Club down to Saltdean. Kelly scratched a head only partially covered with iron grey hair, and said: 'Aaronson? . . . No. Never heard of any Aaronson.'

'No. No more have me canaries.'

'And I never heard of the Mick as a 'chivver,' Herbert. But it's a murder rap. I'll scout round and see what I can turn up.'

It was eleven o'clock when the telephone in the little Poplar sitting-room shrilled. Kelly lifted the ancient receiver. 'That Edward Kelly,' a voice asked. 'Inspector Wolsey of West End. I want you to come up here, pronto.'

'West End? What's up?'

'To put it bluntly over the phone, old timer, we're holding your two kids, and I want you to fetch them home.' The voice was distinctly clear in the room. Kelly held the receiver at arm's length and stared at it as if doubting that words were coming over it.

'What have they done?' he demanded. 'You're meaning Albert and Jackie?'

'You come up here and I'll tell you.'

'C'on, put it down,' Jones said. 'I'll pinch a car from the nick here and drive you up West. We can run 'em home in it afterwards.'

They set off, Kelly crouched in the front passenger seat. 'You ain't got any kids have you, Herbert? Bit of luck for you. I've scraped to bring this pair up and give them a good school when they ought to be working for money, and they goes and gets into the hands of the police — Gawd's truth.'

'Look, son,' Jones comforted. 'They can't have done much if Wolsey wants you to fetch 'em home. They ain't been pinched.'

Kelly was not the only parent roused. People had been called from their homes all over London by phone calls which said 'Come and take your son/daughter home.' The genesis of all this was that time-honoured police phrase — 'From information received, I proceeded.' In this case however, the 'I' was very much plural.

At nine-thirty that evening there left the West End station three police cars, a bus, a Black Maria and twenty assorted police constables and police women. Outside a basement entrance they got out, sealed off the street by placing a bus across it at one end and the Black Maria at the other end. Then they made a sudden and unannounced entrance into the Juventus Youth Club which had been opened three months earlier.

Some sixty teenagers were settling down for an all-night beat and dancing session and were awaiting the arrival of a five-piece dance band. They were staggered by the raid, most of them in panic.

All the youngsters were taken to the West End station in their own interests and for their protection. The adults and club officials were accommodated in the Black Maria. Detectives made a hasty search of the club premises and came away with cigarettes, a large number of tablets, and packets of powder which were taken to a laboratory for examination.

Thirty teenagers of both sexes were sitting disconsolately in the police canteen when Jones and Kelly reached the station. 'Hello, Hello, Super. What's your part in this?' Inspector Wolsey asked of Jones.

'Nuthin'. I wuz with Kelly when you phoned. I nicked a squad car and brought him in. What's been goin' on?' The inspector told them.

'And my kids were in this?' Kelly asked.

'Right. They're in the canteen.'

'Fetch 'em out. Drugs? You want information? I'll get it if I have to beat it out of them?'

'Well, don't do it here. Get them home first.'

The two were brought in. Kelly eyed them in silence for a few minutes. Then:

'Forty years I was a police officer with a first class conduct record. A good father, too. And now I have to be disgraced by having to bail out my children taken in a drug raid on a vicious night club. And in front of my fellow police officers.' He turned to the inspector. 'Have they been searched?'

'No, Sergeant.'

'Turn your pockets out on the table, and you your handbag.' He watched them and seized on a packet of cigarettes and opened it. Two were missing. 'Smoked them?' he asked and received a nod. Jones examined the remaining cigarettes. They were made of coarse strands of brown tobacco loosely packed. The packet bore no brand or name. He sniffed at the cigarettes. 'Where'd you buy them, son?' he asked.

'I didn't buy them Father; they were given me in the club.'

'Given free, gratis?'

'Yes. Why not? Several of the fellows received a packet to try, and see if they liked them.'

Inspector Wolsey held out a hand, was

118

given the packet, and examined it very briefly. 'Given you by one in there?' he demanded pointing to the end section of the canteen. 'Which of them was it?' There was no reply.

'He's waiting, Albert,' Kelly said.

'I'm not narking,' the boy said. 'We're all in it.'

Kelly stepped forward, lifted a hand and with a blow sent the lad staggering across the room. 'You're narking, m'lad. Come on or I'll land you one all the way home.' He jerked him in the direction of the men. 'Which one was it?'

The boy pointed to one of the men. 'Right,' Kelly said. 'Now get back to your sister.'

The inspector consulted a list and walked up to the man. 'You are William Salmon, I see. You saw the boy point you out. I'm now charging you, Salmon, with being in possession of the drug *cannabis Indica*, known as marihuana, and having dealings in it.' He was taken to the cells.

'What about my boy?' Kelly asked. 'In possession.'

'Unknowingly. Forget it. Take him

119

home and the girl and keep them away from night clubs.'

'They'll be kept away from night anythin's.' He looked at them. 'You'll be home every night at seven o'clock, and you'll stay home. If you don't I'll knock you both into the middle of next week.'

17

Doctor Manson heard this story from Jones in the middle of the morning. Meanwhile, Jones in his search for detail had acquired additional knowledge. William Salmon who by this time had appeared before a magistrate and been remanded in custody had, Jones discovered, associations with two other clubs, including the Inferno. After a few moments' consideration the Doctor dialled the Narcotics branch of the Yard. 'The tablets and powder seized in the raid on the Juventus Club — have they been analysed?' he asked.

'Yes, Commander. There was LSD, opium, a little heroin and morphine and some marihuana.'

Manson saw what he thought was a pattern working; only a slight, nebulous pattern, but still a pattern. Drugs had been at large in the Juventus Club and marihuana was distributed in a few cigarettes among teenagers. An associate of the Juventus was a leading figure in the Inferno Night Club, resort of older people, particularly those who frequented night clubs generally. Was there, he wondered, a planned conspiracy among purveyors of drugs to promote drug-taking among teenagers, so that they became addicts and resorted to known sources of supply; the most likely would be, of course, night clubs.

Aaronson was, or had been, a member of the Inferno and had supplies of heroin in the Water Street hovel. Drugs seemed to be a link between all three. He decided that Kenway had better be well briefed before he paid any visits. The plan was halted by an unexpected development which occurred at Worthing. News of the discovery of Slasher Moore stabbed to death at Brighton, eleven miles away, had appeared in due course in the *Argus*, the local evening paper. The report was seen next morning in a copy picked out of a wastepaper receptacle in the municipal gardens bordering the sea front, by an individual who presented the appearance of having slept rough for several nights.

A quarter of an hour later he charged, panting, into the charge room of a local police station and stood with his mouth opening and shutting, but without any words coming out. The charge sergeant pushed him on to a bench. 'What the hell's biting you — coming shoving in here like this?' he demanded.

The man found his voice with an effort. 'For God's sake shove me in the nick,' he shouted: a demand that brought an astonished 'What!' from the sergeant who was more accustomed to the demand 'let me outa here.'

'Take it easy, man,' he said. 'Why in thunder do you want to be locked up? Your missus after you?' He giggled, but the joke fell flat.

'He's going to murder me. Lock me up.' The man was twisting his cap in his fingers, and shaking with fright. The sergeant, leaving a constable in charge of the desk, hauled him into an interviewing room and stood over him. 'Now, let's have it,' he said. 'Somebody is going to murder you. Who?'

'I dunno.'

'Why's he going to murder you?'

'I dunno. I ain't done nuthin'.'

'You don't know! Then how do you know he's going to do you in?'

'It's all in the paper.' He found himself holding up the crunched-up page of the *Argus*, and held it out. 'Here, see.'

'What! He's advertising it? You don't know who he is. You don't know where he is, and you haven't done anything. Why's he after your blood?'

'Because I knows him.'

'You've just said you don't know him.'

'I means I'd know him if I see'd him. He's killed me mate. He'd have know'd him, too. And I'm the only one left as would.'

'Now look, old man,' the sergeant said, 'you go home and have a sleep and you'll be all right afterwards, and don't come back here disturbing the peace with fairy stories.'

'I ain't goin'. I want to be safe inside where he can't get me. I'll heave a brick through your flaming windows, if you chuck me out.' There was no doubt that the man was frightened. The sergeant eyed him — and stark terror at the thought of walking out into the street again was pictured in his eyes. He called a constable. 'Dawkins,' he said, 'stay with this man while I have a word with the C.I.D.'

Detective Inspector Woodhouse listened to the sergeant's story and went downstairs to the interview room. 'Now, what's all this about?' he demanded. 'If you're in any danger man, we'll look after you. You've told the sergeant that someone you don't know is going to murder you for doing nothing.'

'He's done in me mate, guv'nor, and he'll be after me.'

The inspector rubbed his chin. 'Let's start at the beginning, shall we? What's your name?'

'Monrose, Nicholas Monrose.'

'And your address?'

'I ain't got no address.'

'You say the man you don't know has done in your mate. What was your mate's name?'

'Bill Moore. Us called him Slasher Moore.'

'What!' The inspector jumped like a startled faun. He went out of the room to return with a copy of the *Argus*. 'You mean it was your friend who was found stabbed at Saltdean?' The man nodded. 'You were with him in Brighton?'

'I wuz until the day afore yesterday. Then we got scared and parted. I come down here.'

The inspector had a talk with Chief Inspector Perry at Brighton, who intimated that he wanted nothing to do with Monrose, but that Scotland Yard did. 'You get into touch with Commander Doctor Manson,' he said. 'He wants your man very badly.'

Doctor Manson agreed that he wanted to see the man. He would, he said, send down a couple of men to pick him up. Inspector Woodhouse went back to Monrose. 'You're in luck,' he told him. 'We are going to keep you until Scotland Yard comes for you.'

Superintendent Jones and a sergeant were in Worthing within two hours. 'I've come for The Mick,' the Fat Man said.

'The Mick?' Woodhouse looked puzzled.

'Nick Monrose.'

'You know him, Superintendent?'

Jones leaned forward, mockingly confidential. 'Known him for years, Inspector. One of our regular clients. Keeps East End flatties in their jobs. There'd be redundancies without 'im. He's damn near got a charge book all to hisself. Where is he?' The inspector, thinking to himself that they had some very peculiar people among the tops of Scotland Yard (he'd never struck anybody quite like Old Fat Man), took him downstairs. Monrose was brought up from the cells. He took one look at his visitor.

'Gawd, am I glad to see you, Mister Jones,' he said — and meant it.

'Gor blimey,' breathed Jones, '*You* glad ter see *me* . . . to be nicked agen. Now I've heard everything. You . . . ' Words failed him.

'He's been insisting on being locked up ever since we had him,' the inspector put in. 'Said if we didn't take him in, he'd hurl bricks through our windows.'

'And you,' Jones said to Monrose, 'an'

you holidaying at the seaside.'

Three hours later Jones, grumbling ferociously at traffic congestion, traffic lights and speed cops, landed Monrose in Doctor Manson's arms after Jones had given him a précis of the Worthing episode.

'Who's after you, Monrose?' the Doctor asked.

'I don't know, guv'nor.' He saw the doubt in the Doctor's face. 'Honest, guv'nor, I ain't kidding.'

'Who killed the Slasher?'

'I don't know.'

'Well then, who killed Aaronson in Water Street? The Slasher, or you?'

Monrose screamed. 'We never . . . no . . . never. My God, we never. He wor dead when we went in.' A thought struck him. 'How you know we wuz there, anyhow?'

'You had a lot of trouble getting Aaronson through the door, didn't you? He nearly dropped out of your hold and you had to catch at the door lintel. You both left your fingerprints. Now, let's have it from the beginning.'

'An' if it ain't a proper telling I'll 'out' you meself,' Jones said menacingly. 'An' there won't be any witnesses.'

'There is a charge of murder somewhere in the offing,' Manson pointed out.

'Cut me throat if I tells a lie,' Monrose began. 'Slasher an' me was in a pub — '

'What pub — ?' from Jones.

'Navigation Inn, Wapping. We had a couple of half-pints an' then we goes aht. We hadn't bin gone more'n half-way down the street when a bloke heaves up alongside an' says would we like to cop fifty nicker, fer abaht ten minutes work — '

'And you says not arf,' Jones interrupted, 'God darn it, you'd rob your own grandmother for half a dollar. What did he want you to do?'

'You ain't got no right ter say — ' He caught sight of Jones's face and left the sentence unfinished. 'He says as how he's been with a bloke on business and the bloke had conked aht wi' inside haemorrhage. He wuz lyin' on the floor and this bloke wanted us to git him aht an' shove him somewheres else 'cos it wouldn't do fer him to be found dead in the 'ouse — '

'Oh, my gawd,' Jones said. 'He was looking for mugs, and by Hades he found 'em. Go on.'

'He says as the best way was to walk him a'tween us as if he wur sozzled stiff.'

At this Jones's face was a picture of astonishment, and even Doctor Manson looked bewildered at this example of human credulity. 'An' you coupl'a crooks said yes?' Jones waved a hand.

'He says as the old woman who looked arter the ouse'd be in bed and there'd be nobody abaht at two o'clock in the morning — '

'So you went in, hiked Aaronson out, leaving your dabs all over the place, you ruddy mugs. Where'd you dump him?'

'In a derelict barge in a corner of The Basin as this bloke know'd of. He says when he's found there the bogies 'ud think as he crept in there for a kip and died in his sleep. That is if he wuz ever found.'

Doctor Manson was about to speak when Jones held up a hand. The superintendent leaned forward on his chair and pushed his face close up to that of Monrose. 'An' that's all you did, is it, Mick, just moved a stiff? Then why you and Slasher are like a coupla scared cats, an' why does Slasher get hisself knifed and you want locking up 'cos somebody's arter you with that same knife? Let's hear about that, me hearty?'

Monrose swallowed hard, his Adam's apple going up and down like, as Jones said later to Kenway, a ruddy Yo-Yo. He ran a finger round the inside of his neckerchief. 'When we gets the stiff inside the barge, Mister Jones, Slasher says we might as well make him nice and comfortable so as it'd be like the bloke said as he'd gone in for a kip. He unfastens his jacket and slips a hand inside — '

'Lookin' for his wallet, o' course.'

'The stiff was wearin' only a shirt, an' we sees as he's been stabbed — outed.' He gulped again. 'When we comes out we wuz shocked-like. The bloke pays us the twenty-five nicker — '

'Thought you said fifty?'

'He'd forked out half afore we started.

Oh, he says, what's the matter wiz you. We says we don't like lookin' at corpses, and orf we goes. The bloke goes in the barge to see as we've done it properly.'

'Oh, my gawd,' Jones ejaculated, 'an' he twigs you've twigged the knifing an' reckons you'd know him again 'avin' been talking to him face to face.'

'We see'd him tailing us next day when we wuz on a buildin' job. Then we hears as 'ow a big fat bastard was inquiring abaht us from the foreman — '

'That was *me*,' Jones roared. He sat up in his chair, legs apart and hands on his knees. He beamed benevolence. 'It's a good spiel you're givin' us, Mick,' he said. 'You orter be a novelist with a plot like that. Your dabs on the door and nobody else's. 'Ow about you and Slasher knifin' the feller, pinchin' his money and hiding the misdeed in the barge, eh?'

Monrose yelped in fright. He fell back in his chair and nearly fainted. 'We never . . . we never,' he shouted. A sergeant poked his head round the door to see what the row was about. Jones waved him away. 'He's a bit excited,' he explained.

'We never see the stiff afore,' Monrose said. A thought struck him and a slight grin broke over his face. 'If us did it, why was Slasher knocked off, copper?'

'Dick, you ignorant no-good. Dick. How about me telling the tale for a change? You and Slasher outs Aaronson, pockets his dough, gives some to your molls and hops it with the rest. You're the only witness against Slasher and he's the only witness against you if you is both copped. So you both plays cat and mouse and it's you as wins, and Slasher is outed.'

Monrose's yell of protest rose to a scream. He jumped up, waved his arms in the air and was practically incoherent. 'Me . . . me . . . ' he shouted when he found his voice. 'I couldn't kill a bloody mouse — '

'Course you couldn't catch one,' Jones said.

'It's like I told you, strike me dead if it ain't.'

'C'on!' Jones said.

'You goin' ter lock me up?'

'We're goin' to see the unfortunate laddie takin' a long kip in that barge.'

They went down to Wapping in two cars. Doctor Manson and Jones in one with a surgeon and two constables and Monrose in the other. A call was made at Wapping headquarters to pick up a local inspector and an ambulance.

The barge lay derelict and rotting away at the edge of a disused wharf at the top end of the Basin. It had laid there, the local inspector said, for years and had at one time been the favourite playground for the boys of the neighbourhood until a child was drowned after falling in the bilge. Then it was placed out of bounds.

The body of the man was in the cabin. Moore and Monrose, Doctor Manson noted, had conveyed an excellent impression of a down and out who had crept into the barge for shelter. It lay on its back, had a sack as a pillow and another rotting sack over the legs. Getting the body out proved a difficult and disagreeable task necessitating it being strapped on to a stretcher which then had to be upended to enable it to be passed out through the hatchway to the deck.

In the mortuary, Doctor Manson and the Divisional Surgeon conducted a post mortem examination. The stab seemed to have been made with a knife, the blade of which had a width of one and a half inches at its broadest part. The single stab had gone straight through the heart and, the surgeon said, would have caused instant death.

Manson examined closely the forearms of the body, frowned and did the same with the thighs. 'Odd,' he said quietly; and the surgeon looked inquiringly. 'I thought to find hypodermic marks,' the Doctor said. He was recalling the tablets, spoon and eye dropper and needle found in the Water Street attic loft.

'Who is he, anyway?' the surgeon asked, and received the answer: 'We don't know other than that his name is Aaronson and that he seems to have been in the habit of disguising himself and going about secretly.'

He was wrong! Jones, at that moment was on his way to the old hag who looked after the Water Street house. He found her where he had last seen her — sitting on the top step outside the front door. She recognised him as he came forward. 'It ain't no good goin' up,' she called remembering the previous altercation. 'He ain't been here for days and his money's due tomorrer.'

'He won't be coming, Missus.' Jones broke the news. 'He's dead.'

'Dead! . . . Dead is he . . . The bastard. What about the rent?' she screamed. 'I'll ha' to pay it. Had he got any money on him?'

'Shouldn't think so, judging by where we found him. You come along 'o me and see. We want you to identify him. You're the only one we know ever to have seen him. What's your name?'

'Giles, copper; Sarah Giles and there's nobody can say as I ain't got a good reputation.'

At Wapping police headquarters Mrs. Giles was taken into the mortuary. 'Mrs. Giles, Doctor,' Jones introduced. 'She'll identify Aaronson for us.'

'Very good of you Mrs. Giles,' the Doctor said.

The sheet was pulled back from the face and Sarah stepped forward, morbid excitement lighting up her own face.

She looked and then turned round in a fury.

'What's the bloody game, copper?' she burst out. 'You said as 'ow he were dead.'

'Well, ain't he?' Jones said. 'He's deader 'n mutton.'

'Him? Aye, *he's* dead right enough. Only he ain't Aaronson — a little runt like that. Aaronson was a strong man.'

'Then who in 'ell is this?'

'How should I know, copper. I ain't never seen him afore. What made you think he was Aaronson?'

'Because a couple of characters carried him out'a Aaronson's rooms in your hovel, Missus, where he was stabbed to death, that's why.'

'It's a flamin' lie. I never see'd nobody go in an' they has ter pass me.'

'You wouldn't have seen anybody. It was two o'clock in the morning. You want to lock that front door o' yours at night, Missus, or you'll wake up one morning and find yourself dead.'

18

'Do you believe him?' the A.C. asked. He had listened to the story of Monrose, of the night's adventures, of the body, and of the Slasher. It was of Monrose that he was speaking.

'As a matter of fact, I do,' Doctor Manson said. 'The man is terrified — and he couldn't invent that.'

'You're keeping him inside?'

'Oh, yes. He has been charged with concealment of death, breaking and entering and obstructing the police in their inquiries. That should keep him inside for quite a time. We'll guard him well and truly. He's the only living soul we know who can identify the man who killed in the attic.' He grinned. 'I nearly said who killed Aaronson.'

'I suppose the woman isn't lying in not identifying the body as Aaronson's?'

'You wouldn't think so, had you seen her. She's scouring the East End for him and a week's rent. The physique as described by her earlier certainly doesn't fit the body in the barge.'

'And there is no trace of the real Aaronson?'

'Not a vestige.'

'Nor of the body we have?'

'Nor of that. We hope something may turn up after we've issued an appeal through the Press. Somebody must have missed him.' He consulted a paper and read it out aloud:

'A man was found dead in a house in Water Street, Wapping and has so far not been identified. He was aged about sixty, and was five feet seven inches in height, of slim build, with brown hair and hazel eyes. He was dressed in a dark grey jacket and trousers and a blue vest. Anyone who can give information is asked to communicate with New Scotland Yard, or any police station.'

'If the body isn't Aaronson,' the A.C. said slowly, 'then Aaronson is presumably alive. He may appear himself in answer to the appeal.'

'Not at all likely, Edward, if he thinks the man was killed in his room in mistake for himself.'

(It may be said here that nobody came forward in answer to the appeal and the identity of the murdered man is unknown to this day.)

The A.C. was fiddling with a gold pencil and avoiding the eyes of the Doctor: who asked, 'What's on your mind, Edward?'

'Something I don't like the sound of, Harry — Monrose's description of the man who accosted him and the Slasher with fifty pounds 'a big strong man'; and Jones's theory of what was likely to happen to one who snuffed out a member of a mob. Barstowe, as we both know, was a big strong man. Suppose he killed a man he thought was Aaronson — bear in mind that Barstowe seems to have been in Water Street for he had a receipt made out to Aaronson for that room — well,

Barstowe was killed, too.'

'I know. I've been thinking on the same lines. I think we've got to find Aaronson. We've a line that should prove something.'

'How come?'

'He was a member of the Inferno Club. Somebody there must know something about him. We'll get Kenway in there, incognito — as a member.'

'Club — yes. What's happening about the Juventus?'

'Charges against the adults. Nothing against the teenagers except a suggestion to the parents that they should exercise more discipline. The club will be struck off.'

Kenway, well briefed by the Doctor, made his first visit to the club that night. The Inferno Club is contained in a cellar basement underneath a block of shops with offices above in the heart of the West End. In the gay days of the early thirties it had been an expensive and select night club, lavishly furnished, entry into which had necessitated evening dress — not just a dinner jacket. In those days it opened at eleven p.m. and ran until four o'clock in the morning when bacon and eggs were served on tables which had held champagne during most of the night. The outbreak of the Second World War killed it, as it did most of Bohemia in London, and the graciousness of life that made London so pleasant a place in which to live. The premises then lapsed into a cellar again until, with the advent of 'You've Never Had It So Good' era it was taken over by a small group of men, and became once more a night club.

A narrow set of stairs from the street led down to its real entrance. In the old days the stairs had been carpeted; but not now. Nor was there a handrail. Inspector Kenway walked down the stairs. In a small glass-fronted cubby-hole alongside one wall of a square lobby sat a woman neatly dressed in black with white facings. She had a mass of hair piled high on her head; Kenway had the thought that there was probably a 'cage' underneath it to make the height.

She looked up as he reached the window and eyed him closely. 'Are you a member, sir?' she asked.

'No. I'm afraid not. But I want to get in.'

'That will be all right, sir. The entrance fee is three guineas. I can give you a membership application form which you can sign. What name?'

'Reginald Emerson. But I don't know any member to propose me.'

'Oh, that's all right. I can arrange that, and a seconder.' She wrote the name on a card similar to that which had been found in Aaronson's loft refuge. 'If you will please put your name at the bottom, sir,' she asked, 'you will, of course, come in free in future. You can order any drinks you like inside. I should point out that we do not accept cheques in payment.'

Kenway smiled. 'Who does? How about dancing?'

'You will find plenty of partners.' She pressed a button, and a uniformed attendant appeared. 'A new member, Fred. See that he is introduced.' Inside, he was shown to a vacant table. 'Can I get you a drink, sir?' his escort asked. 'Sure. I'd like a large whisky and soda.' It came;

and he now had time to inspect the club.

It was a very large, square room apparently covering the foundations of the entire street block. Tables for two or four were scattered round the outside of a small dancing square. The lighting was dim, almost dark, and came from red candle-lights set in the middle of each table. The only white lighting came from the lights on the music stands of the dance band set on a platform about midway along the length of the room. It was a four-piece orchestra — violin, saxophone, piano and drums.

Over the orchestra platform was a huge statue in cardboard or some material, of the Devil, lit by red lights which flickered on and off. The walls of the club were decorated with mural paintings of scenes from Dante's *Inferno*. The waitresses were dressed in red with black caps and had forked 'tails' attached behind. Grotesque, Kenway said to himself, was hardly an adequate description. The dance floor at the moment was occupied by a dozen or so couples moving round in no apparent pattern, but including any step that came into their minds.

Seeing clearly was a little difficult in the gloom, but peering round Kenway noticed a woman sitting on a stool at the bar. She was wearing a mini-skirt which, from the way she was sitting, exposed an expanse of nylon stocking well past her thighs. As though feeling she was being looked at she glanced up and caught his eyes as he glanced at her legs — and smiled. After a moment or two she slid off the stool and started to weave a way between the dancers, ending up at his table. Kenway drew out a chair for her. 'Thank you,' she acknowledged, and sat down.

Kenway placed her as one of the professional hostesses attached to all night clubs either as employees or, more often, as freelances drawing a commission on expensive drinks which they can induce patrons to buy, and on 'presents' which the same members offer for dancing partnerships.

'I thought you looked a little lonely,' she said. 'I don't remember seeing you before, so I thought I would introduce myself.'

'It *is* my first visit.' Kenway smiled.

'Really! I think you will find the entertainment and the company very pleasant. Would you like me to sit with you a little while and point out some of the regular customers you may like to meet?'

'That would be most kind of you.' He moved his chair round to be at her side, and she suggested, 'Would you like to buy me a drink?'

'You took the words out of my mouth. What would you like?'

'A bottle of champagne would be very nice. Incidentally, they do not rook members on the prices here.'

One of the red-tailed waitresses brought and opened the bottle. Kenway and the hostess clinked glasses. 'Fortune!' he said.

'Fortune. I'm Margaret, what is your name?'

'Reginald . . . Reginald Emerson.'

'I'll call you Reggie. Good evening, Reggie.'

'Good evening, Margaret. Pleased to know you.' They clinked glasses again. She pointed out several people. The big man standing by the door marked 'toilets' she said is the manager, Petersen. 'Who introduced you, Reggie?' she asked.

'Nobody. I said I wanted to come in and the girl in the box took three pounds off me in exchange for a membership card.'

'Oh yes. What made you want to join?'

'Somewhere to come at night when I am in London. Actually, I am expecting to meet someone I know here. He said he was usually in the club at night. Fellow named Aaronson.'

'Jacob? Oh, yes. I know him. He knows a lot of people here, but mostly Hookey.'

'Hookey?'

'The fiddler in the band. Jacob hasn't been in for a week now, which is most unusual. I was wondering what had happened to him. Perhaps he's ill. Do you know him well?'

'Lord, no. Just casually. We met in a pub, got talking and he suggested I came here. He said I'd find him here. I expect he'll turn up some time. Shall we dance?'

They did a few turns round the dance square and then resumed their seats. The manager wandering round the room, stopping occasionally at various tables exchanging greetings, reached them and patted Margaret on the shoulders. 'Good evening, Margaret,' he greeted. She smiled an answer; 'Oh, Mr. Petersen, meet Reggie, a new member on his first visit.'

'Ah, yes. I have just signed as proposer his application form. We are pleased to have you. I am sure that Margaret will see you comfortable.'

With a loud, discordant clash the band finished and the floor emptied. Kenway felt an air of expectancy running through the club, and was puzzled for the reason. Margaret turned towards him. 'Hookey is going to do his solo number now, Reggie. It's usually marvellous.'

The violinist stepped forward, placed his instrument under his chin, waved the bow and began to play. Kenway who had lolled back in his chair suddenly sat up and began to take notice. Music poured wildly, almost indecently from the instrument; music that out-gypsied the wildest gypsy music he had ever heard. The violin laughed, shrieked, swore and cried, the player performing sensual antics as he bowed. Now and then the drums crashed and rolled, sounds which seemed to excite the player to greater efforts.

'What on earth is it?' Kenway asked.

'His own composition, Reggie. He calls it 'Dark Nights'.' Kenway thought to himself that terror nights would have been more applicable. The condition of the player emphasised the description. Sweat was pouring down his face and dropping off; his eyes staring ahead seemed to see nothing of the room. A clash of cymbals and drums ended the performance, and the violinist bowed to a tremendous burst of applause. He stood wiping with a handkerchief the sweat gleaming on his forehead and cheeks. His hands were shaking and his mouth twitching. The drummer clapped him on the shoulder, and he turned, bowed again, walked to the door marked 'toilets' and went through.

'Amazing,' Kenway said. 'Is that a nightly performance?'

'Not always. But very often about this time.'

The band struck up for dancing again, but only with piano, sax and drums. After about ten minutes the violinist emerged from a door and on the stand took up his violin again. He was no longer sweating, his hands had lost their shaking and his mouth the twitch; his eyes were smiling as he signalled to the band.

Margaret had disappeared to repair her make-up. Hookey presently laid down his violin, leaving the other instruments to carry on, walked across to Kenway's table and sat down. 'Do you mind, sir?' he asked.

'Be my guest,' Kenway said. 'May I say that was a brilliant performance you gave?'

'Nice of you to say so.' Kenway signalled a waitress. 'Champagne,' he said and held out a cigarette case.

'No. Have one of mine,' Hookey invited snapping open a gold case. 'You may like them better.' Kenway took one and

150

Hookey flicked open a lighter for it and his own cigarette. Kenway inhaled; the cigarette, he realised, was marihuana. 'A satisfactory flavour,' he said.

'Margaret tells me you are a friend of Aaronson, sir.'

Kenway spread a hand. 'I wouldn't go that far. A mere acquaintance. I sat next to him in a hotel bar. Actually I was on my way to Manchester after doing business in London.'

'Manchester?'

'Yes. I'm up and down there about every fortnight, spending three or four nights in London. That's how I come to be in here. Aaronson said it's the best place in London to pass a night away; I should say he's right. I thought he'd be here.'

'Haven't seen him for several days now.'

'Oh well, I expect he'll turn up soon.'

Margaret returned looking refreshed. 'He's all yours,' Hookey told her and returned to the band. It was two o'clock in the morning before Kenway left for home. His offer to see Margaret to her flat was regretfully declined. 'I'd like to, Reggie,' she said, 'but I have to stay until the club closes — and that is when the company present is too few in numbers to be profitable.'

At the door on the way out the manager met him. 'Enjoyed yourself?' he asked, and Kenway nodded. 'Perfectly,' he said.

'Well, I hope we shall see you regularly. If there should be anything you *particularly* want, *do* please come to me *personally*.'

19

'It's a very queer nightie,' Kenway said, reporting to Doctor Manson later in the morning. The Doctor had listened intently for some minutes to a full story of the club; and now sat silent, with creases in the corners of his eyes and lines across the broad high forehead. They betokened puzzlement over a problem. He opened his eyes at last. 'The club was orderly?' he asked.

'Quite. No excitement. Normal night club behaviour. The only incident was the extraordinary playing of the violinist. Do you know something, Doctor? I had the idea that he'd taken a shot of drug — say LSD.'

'Lysergic acid diethylamide?' The Doctor shook his head.

'How come you don't think so? From what I have read a shot of it seems to lead to scenes like that.'

'I arrive at the decision from your

description of the way he came back after the performance, Kenway. He was normal in behaviour earlier on and before the solo effort?'

'Quite. In fact he is a very good musician.'

'And he returned to the stand after his phenomenal playing and was as he had been before?'

'That's so. It was then that he came over to me. By the way the cigarette he offered and which I smoked was mari-huana — and stronger than any I've smoked before.'

'There's nothing we can do about that. He wasn't selling or pushing them. No, the point I want to make is that if he returned in normal behaviour after twenty minutes, or less, he hadn't taken LSD. Even a small trip of the stuff will give the taker up to eighteen hours of hallucinations, and never less than six hours.' He communed with himself for a few moments. 'I am inclined to think that had he come to the end of a sniffing or 'shot' of heroin, a fact which sends an addict into a state of frenzy, making him sweat profusely and producing unnatural efforts. A hypodermic injection of heroin would have him back to normal in a quarter of an hour.'

'You mean he's hooked on heroin, Doctor?'

'You might ask your lady friend why he is known as Hookey. Tell me Kenway, how was he dressed?'

'Baggy trousers, loose silk shirt — like a Hungarian gypsy.'

'Long sleeves with tight cuffs.'

'Yes. How did you know?'

'Hiding hypodermic marks on the forearms probably. They can't be disguised. We can't do anything about that at the moment. Anything else?'

Kenway drew his brows together. 'Come to think back, Doctor,' he said, slowly, 'there is one odd point. I followed our line that Aaronson suggested that I join the club and meet him there. Now, Hookey, the manager both asked if I was a friend of Aaronson and so did the girl. They seemed to go out of their way to know all I knew about Aaronson. I stuck to our story.'

Kenway's story worried the Doctor not a little. He did not like the various inquiries into how the detective came to know Aaronson and thus patronise the Inferno Club. After all, Aaronson had been killed or so it was assumed until they found a trace of him. Until they found the body or some evidence of death there was no certainty of that. But, anyway, the man had vanished, and some unidentified person had met death in Aaronson's room.

Had he been mistaken for Aaronson? It was, the Doctor thought, possible. On the other hand, Aaronson could himself have killed the man who might have been trespassing or blackmailing, and then have fled. And who was the burly individual who had paid fifty pounds to get the body of the unknown man out of the room?

'Aaronson himself, his very own self,' Jones suggested. Kenway had scoffed at the idea. 'Where'd a man living in a hovel like that acquire fifty nicker?' he argued. 'If he could pick up money like that why the devil was he living in such surroundings?'

Manson eyed them both. 'Is the Inferno a cheap kind of place, Kenway?' he asked.

'Good lord, no. On the contrary.'

'Then attach yourself to your own argument; how comes it that a man living in the conditions of Water Street comes to frequent, regularly, an expensive night club — as we know he did?

'He knew Hookey and we suggest the violinist to be a drug addict. We found heroin in Water Street. Aaronson was a drug addict.' Kenway stated a case.

'Quarrel over supplies, and a killing?' Jones asked.

The problem was rendered more complex by the fact that despite the inquiries of half a dozen detectives who scoured the East End, and of others searching nearer West, no one could be found who knew Aaronson. The only evidence of his existence was that of the old hag in Water Street, and three or four people, including Margaret, who knew him in the Inferno Club.

Jones had visited the Navigation Inn in Wapping where Nick Monrose said they had been prior to the Slasher and his experience with the stranger who paid fifty pounds for the removal of the corpse. The landlord remembered the two as having been present, and remembered, too, pointing them out as a pair wanting to be watched when the stranger had suggested there might be a rough element in a public house in such an area. He could not say whether the stranger had followed them out, or whether it was chance that he left after them. Nor had he any idea who the customer was. So far as he knew he had never before seen him. That, Jones conceded, supported Monrose's story.

And that was as far as the investigation had gone. Jones's 'narks' and 'canaries', usually mines of information, could find no trace of Aaronson, despite the promise of handsome rewards for information — and no questions asked.

A round-table conference with the A.C. decided that Kenway should continue his visits to the Inferno, and that a detective from an outlying area should gain membership to the club and co-relate

Kenway's observations. The point was not gained without effort. The A.C. had tapped an elegantly chased gold pencil on his pad. There was that appearance about him that suggested a duck miles away from its pool, and looking for it. 'What gentlemen,' he had suggested — and very pertinently 'has all this to do with the murder of Barstowe, in which we are solely interested?'

It was a good question: and took the company several minutes to consider; and then eyes turned on Doctor Manson for an answer. He grimaced. 'The murder of Barstowe *and* the murder of someone we haven't identified,' he pointed out sarcastically. 'Don't overlook that. He's equal in law to Barstowe. Now, Barstowe had a rent receipt made out to Aaronson. He must have got it from the man personally, or from the hole in which the man lived and where it was delivered. Why did he visit Aaronson and the address? Aaronson was a member of the Inferno Club; he was friendly with a known addict who conducts the band in the Inferno. He had in his possession heroin 'caps' and the wherewithal to convert the 'caps' into liquid heroin, and to inject it into his body. The link between all these is heroin and the Inferno. And we have to find out where Barstowe fitted into this link.'

20

Kenway kept clear of the Inferno for some days in support of his story of coming from Manchester to London and staying for several days at a time. He made a reappearance on the fourth night. The club was fairly well filled at ten o'clock with men and women drawn seemingly from every rank of society. Margaret was dancing with a slim man of about thirty years of age, well dressed in a dark suit with white shirt and black bow tie. At a distance in the gloom of the interior he seemed to be wearing a dinner jacket suit. As Kenway skirted the dance floor Margaret signalled to him, drew her partner off the floor and went over to a table. Kenway made his way there.

'Hello, Reggie,' she greeted him. 'Back from Manchester? Do you know I *really* missed you.' Kenway grinned. 'Returned like the proverbial bad penny,' he said, and glanced at her companion. 'Oh, I'm sorry,' she apologised, 'meet Mr. Asherton . . . John . . . a new member. He's in my charge. John . . . Reggie Emerson.' They shook hands. Kenway called for champagne.

Half an hour later after alternate dances, Margaret went off to the Powder Room. Asherton drew his chair alongside that of his companion. 'Inspector Kenway?' he asked. 'I'm Detective Sergeant Mitchell.'

'Yes, I recognised the signs. Better stick to the club names and speak softly. You've been here a couple of nights, I gather. Anything interest you?'

'One or two things. For instance — ' He stopped. 'Look out, here's the girl coming back.' They stood to receive her. Another bottle of champagne appeared. Kenway's eyes were searching, obviously, round the room. 'Looking for something, Reggie?' the girl asked.

'I was wondering whether Aaronson was in, Margaret?'

'We haven't seen him since you were here last. Funny. He was usually here two or three times a week.'

It was an hour later that the manager in

his perambulations found himself at their table. ' 'Evening, Mr. Emerson,' he said, and was introduced to Asherton. 'Been away again?'

'Manchester, as usual. It's good to be back.'

'Margaret looking after both of you? Good. Is there anything *special* you would like?'

'As a matter of fact there is. I'd like a word in your ear.'

'Right. Come into the office.' He led the way. Inside: 'Now what can I do for you?'

Kenway looked embarrassed. 'It's a little difficult,' he said. 'I expected to meet Mr. Aaronson here, you know. He helped me once.'

'In what way?'

'With certain goods, when I ran out. He said he could always get them through contacts in the club. That was really why I took his advice and joined. Now, I don't have any contacts and he doesn't appear to be coming.'

Mr. Petersen rubbed a hand over his chin, and stared rather hard at his companion. 'I understand what you mean, Emerson,' he said, 'but — well look here. It's pretty risky, you know. As the club manager I don't know anything about it. But I may be able to find something. What do you want?'

'A few caps — to last me. I'm not absolutely hooked.'

'I'll see what I can do. It will take me the best part of an hour.'

'I'll hang on.'

Next morning in the laboratory Kenway handed over six small, round tablets to Inspector Merry, the Yard's Deputy Scientist. They were found to contain eighty per cent heroin in the mixture. Each 'cap' had cost Kenway two pounds.

To Doctor Manson and the A.C. an hour later, Sergeant Mitchell, sitting with Kenway, told of the things which had interested him during his three nights in the club. 'Three men seem to sit together at the same table each night,' he said. 'One is a man I recognise as having been in a youth club which was raided at Ruislip. It was to be a surprise entry and

164

to allay suspicion outlying officers in plain clothes were called in. I was one. The club was searched but nothing found. Several of the youths present were found in possession of drugs. They were released when their parents were sent for. When the premises were searched more thoroughly after the club was cleared a packet containing drugs was found in a fireplace which had been found previously to have contained nothing but paper. This man is remembered to have moved to the fireplace and stood with his arm on the mantelpiece. We are certain that he dropped the packet there, but we had not, of course, any evidence.'

'The man was clean, Sergeant?'

'When he was searched earlier, yes sir.'

The A.C. was still expressing a little bewilderment at the tangle in which the Barstowe murder was becoming enmeshed. He turned to the Chief Constable of the Yard. 'Why, Chief, has the Inferno been an object of interest to you?' he asked, turning over a sheaf of reports which covered several months.

'Because, sir, men who have used the

club regularly are men we *suspect* of being engaged in dealing in drugs. But we have no evidence.'

'Kenway obtained heroin there last night. Is that evidence?' The Chief grinned. 'It's evidence that your man has been in possession of drugs that he obtained from somebody who was in the club; but not that the club has dealings in drugs.'

'Forget all that,' Manson said, impatiently. 'We want Kenway and Mitchell in the club. Is it your idea, or rather our idea that the club is a distributing centre for drugs?'

'That, my dear Commander, is what we want to know. In earlier days when the cult was not so widespread the distribution centre was the foot of Nurse Cavell's statue in St. Martin's Place. It was a regular open market. When we tumbled to that it moved to a basement tea room just off the Strand. Today? Well — '

Two nights later, at two a.m. police swooped on the Inferno Club. The denizens were gathered together at one end of the room and searched. On Mr.

Emerson (Inspector Kenway) were found two packets of marihuana cigarettes (thoughtfully provided for him by Scotland Yard earlier in the evening). He was arrested with twelve other members of the club on charges of possessing drugs, including in two cases LSD. A special early sessional hearing was held at Bow Street Court where Kenway was fined fifteen pounds for being in possession of drugs. Police officers, warned, looked the other way and gave no sign that they knew anything about his being a police officer.

The raid was, however, unsatisfactory from the police point of view. No drugs were found on the club premises, despite a close search of the management offices and other rooms connected. The manager, giving evidence, said he knew nothing of any drug addicts using the club, and would not have had them in the place had he any such knowledge. Nor did the club deal in any way with drugs.

When Kenway appeared in the club the same night, he was received warmly by the manager and by Hookey, both of whom extended sympathy to the extent of champagne on the house. It was noted by Hookey that Kenway had denied all knowledge of drugs in spite of the fact that he had been given heroin caps.

In the Yard, Doctor Manson expressed decided satisfaction at the outcome of the raid. In response to the A.C.s raised eyebrows he said with a smile: 'We have inaugurated Kenway, or rather Emerson. He is now recognised as an addict to heroin and marihuana and is, as it were, beyond suspicion by the management.'

21

The United States of America is the biggest market in the world for narcotics. The number of heroin addicts in that country is placed at more than 50,000, and Interpol has stated that to satisfy their demands at least more than half a ton of heroin a year must be available for the black market alone. In 1964 nearly 750 pounds of heroin was seized by the Federal Bureau or Narcotics; two years earlier they had arrested a gang found to have smuggled £35,000,000 worth of drugs into America.

In consequence, the Narcotics Bureau and the United Nations Narcotics Commission keep a watchful eye on those passenger and cargo ships which put into American ports from the East — from Japan, Turkey and China; and on ships which have taken Egypt or Tangier in their voyage. Because the greatest crop of poppies in the world is grown in China;

and at Tietsin there is a body called the Chinese Opium Monopoly Bureau which runs a processing plant for heroin under the control of the Economic Commission of the government, and heroin from this is smuggled into South East Asia through Hong Kong and Macao, and thence into Europe and America. There is nothing that the world police organisation, Interpol, can do about it, because its Charter forbids the touching of any form of political crime, and the Chinese official poppy growing and processing of opium is political.

So the U.S.A. port authorities keep an eagle eye on all imports which have come by way of the East; but not on vessels sailing from Britain — at least, the Customs declarations on such cargoes are accepted after a cursory examination. Which made the affair of the motor cargo vessel, *Invista* (15,000 tons) registered at Southampton, a shock on both sides of the Atlantic.

The *Invista* tied up in New York harbour at seven o'clock in the morning with a cargo varied and general in description. Discharging and unloading begins at nine o'clock. With the *Invista* it proceeded without incident until a net load of wooden cases was held high above the ship's forward hold. At it swung over the quayside a rope holding one corner of the carrying netting suddenly snapped with a report like a shot, and the wooden cases were flung out and on to the quayside. One of the cases burst on impact scattering its contents. Two dockers who had been awaiting its lowering were caught by flying splinters of wood and were badly injured. Help was at once forthcoming, and ambulance men removed the men after treatment had been given. Dockers then proceeded to collect the scattered cargo under the eyes of dockside police officers as a precaution against pilfering.

The contents of the smashed case had been pottery. The fragments were being swept up when a Captain of Detectives noticed a quantity of whitish powder. Since there was nothing that could have been powdered by the crash, he bent down and inspected the powder more closely; wet a finger and carried a fragment of powder to his tongue. Then he jumped. 'Holy Mother,' he said, being like most American cops, Irish. 'Stop! For the love of Mike, leave everything.' He turned to Patrolman McGinty. 'Pat,' he said, 'get the Bureau men down here — pronto. You — ' he pointed to the union boss supervising the unloading — 'Hang up. Shut down.'

'Shucks, Captain, we gotta get the stuff out.' A chorus of angry voices echoed his protests. The Captain swung his stick. 'Any buddy want to object?' he asked.

Three members of the Narcotics Bureau arrived, with extra police. With the debris cordoned off they examined the remains of the pottery and the loose powder. It took only a few minutes to arrive at the decision that the powder was heroin; it took upwards of an hour to get it safely collected and taken to the Bureau's laboratory.

Examination of the lading sheets disclosed that the cargo of which the cases were a part, included three cases of Spode china, a popular import from

Britain. A search in the forward hold produced the remaining two cases. They were lifted out, packed on a lorry and taken to the laboratory for investigation. Opened there, they were found to contain Spode china as described. Bureau officers examined the pottery piece by piece and found that among them were a number of vessels closely resembling Spode but which were pseudo and slightly different in shape from the traditional, obviously to make identification certain and quick. All the articles in the cases had been stuffed with cotton wool inside and between them to ensure against damage from knocking or vibration. The filling in the pseudo pieces, however, covered only an inch or so of the depth. Since to any ordinary glance they would show no difference from the other pieces, and since they had been packed in the middle or at the bottom of the cases, it was likely that had there been any close Customs examination they would have been easily overlooked.

The inch or so of cotton wool removed,

the contents of the articles — three-quarters of the entire depth of each piece — were found to be filled with wrapped packets of heroin, or heroin powder carefully wrapped in special wrapping. In all, the laboratory extracted no less than forty-five pounds of heroin, the biggest amount ever recovered in a single haul. The fact was carried to the Police Commissioner enthroned in 240, Centre Street, the 19th Century Baroque building which is the headquarters of the New York Police. He had the Chief Inspector with him, and heard of the discovery with astonishment spilling out from his face and with his mouth opening and shutting without any sound coming from it for several moments. Then:

'Jees!' he said. 'What's it worth?'

'Somewhere over and above two million dollars,' a member of the Narcotics Bureau said in hushed tones. 'That is in the neighbourhood of £700,000.' He added, 'In the black market, of course.'

'Get busy,' the Commissioner said. The chief inspector grimaced. Fighting the 'boss' of the drug ring in New York is like trying to pick up a needle out of a bundle of hay. He started with the Bill of Lading of the consigned cargo. The cases had been addressed to Simon Grudelberger, to await collection at the docks. The consignors had been A. Abrahams and Co., Ltd., of Liverpool Street, Rotherhithe, London.

A delve into records showed earlier imports to a Gunsberg and Solomon, and a Knickerbocker, all consigned by Abrahams and Co., and passed through the Customs at New York docks.

'What we're going to do?' the Chief Inspector queried.

'Nothing, nothing at all,' the Chief of Detectives said. 'Just wait and see.'

Three days later Mr. Grudelberger turned up at the docks with a consignment notification and a two-ton van. 'Collectin' three cases,' he announced. 'Pottery. Was it here yet?'

'Come inside,' a Customs Officer invited.

Nobody could have shown more surprise — astonishment is perhaps the better word — than did Mr. Grudelberger when the situation was explained to him, and the result of the laboratory examination was placed before his very eyes. He knew nothing, he said, of anything other than a consignment of pottery and china, commodities in which he dealt, among other things, as an importing agent. Spode, he pointed out, was a fashionable commodity which sold well in the United States. His customers? Anyone, he said, could request him to receive on their behalf imported goods and he had, in fact, been in business that way over a period of years. The consignors in the present unfortunate case was a London firm with whom he had had many dealings. The offer of the china had been made to him and, after trade inquiries, he had found that there was a demand for such ware in the ceramic industry. He had, in fact, received many inquiries after he had written to London.

'Who made the offer to you?' the Chief of Detectives asked.

'Abrahams and Company, of London.'

Now, the tough police guys of New

York have not the fastidiousness of London 'dicks'. Nor are they bound and hampered by such fool devices as 'a man is innocent until he is proved guilty', or by certain Judges' Rules; they possess and use certain 'persuaders'. One such is a powerful light shining into a suspect's eyes; another consists of a rubber truncheon or stick.

'Bum, a company don't sign no letters,' the Captain explained to Mr. Grudelberger. 'Who made the offer?'

A rubber truncheon restored the lapsed memory of Mr. Grudelberger as to who was the actual signer of the letter which he had, most unfortunately lost. After three applications of that *aide memoir* he remembered that the letter had been signed by a Mr. Maddison.

Further persuasion brought to his recollection that he knew something of the possible contents of certain articles in the cases (apart from genuine pottery) but there had been nothing he could do about it, being under pressure from a drug syndicate. No persuasion of any kind could get out of him the name of the

'Boss', or of any other leaders of the syndicate: not even treatment from investigating officers which landed him in a prison infirmary. A sympathetic police chief appreciated the reason — nobody wants to sign his own death warrant.

En passant: A Federal Judge sent Grudelberger to gaol. He lasted two months in prison: then was mysteriously attacked and killed. The prison authorities made little investigation into the circumstances. They wouldn't have found out anything; and anyway, in police circles in New York it is best not to inquire too closely into things like that.

22

'Two men have been murdered, A.C.,' Doctor Manson said, 'and investigations into murder go on without any Statute of Limitations; go on until the murderer is in the dock. Bear that in mind, will you?'

The Assistant Commissioner, harassed by the Receiver because of the expense being incurred by Kenway and Sergeant Mitchell in their nocturnal club life without any obvious result, was critical of the methods of his Homicide Squad. 'Agreed,' he said in reply, 'but why the Inferno? What are they gaining there?'

'Why? Because that is the only association we have with Aaronson, and Aaronson is the only contact we have with Barstowe. Barstowe knew Aaronson. He must have known him to have in his possession a receipt for Aaronson's rent. The only people we can find who knew Aaronson are in the Inferno Club. The violinist there knew him, the girl Margaret knew him, and half a dozen members also knew him, and nobody outside the club did know him, so far as we can trace. He hasn't been seen since the odd affair in Water Street.'

'I ain't surprised,' Jones said. The company turned their eyes on Old Fat Man sitting like a great fat Buddha at the end of the table. 'Ain't it obvious,' he went on, 'as Aaronson killed the fellow an' he's on the run. He's not going to turn up at the Inferno, not unless he's stark raving bonkers.'

'We're keeping Water Street under the rose, you know,' the Chief Constable said. 'What about putting out a general wanted call?'

'Lumme, what on?' Jones roared. 'We ain't got a photograph. We ain't even got a description except the old harridan's statement that the stiff in the barge wasn't Aaronson because he was a little man and Aaronson was a big man. Stone the crows! 'Wanted for murder, a big man.' We'd have a third of the male population of the country in for questioning.'

'You reckon the man in the pub with fifty quid was Aaronson, Fatty?' Kenway asked.

'Well, he knew the body was there, didn't he?'

'He did,' Manson agreed; 'but he wasn't Aaronson.'

'How come not?'

'Sounds reasonable to me,' the Chief Constable said. 'Why shouldn't it be he?'

'Then why in the name of common sense *does he go out of his way to draw attention to the fact by engaging a couple of crooks to remove the body?* Why not, after he had killed, just vanish? The owner of the premises had never seen him; the old hag never went up to the room. The body could have lain there for heaven knows how long before being found. But no; he says there's a body in my room, come and get it away and here's fifty pounds for doing it.'

'An' then he follows 'em round and knocks off one in Brighton and is after the other. Why — if he isn't Aaronson?'

'I don't know,' Manson admitted. 'It's just that sixth sense of mine.'

The conference had been called to report progress. — and it ended as barren as Old Mother Hubbard's cupboard. 'There doesn't seem to be any,' the A.C. said.

'Not quite so,' Manson protested. 'Aaronson and heroin and the Inferno and heroin, and the Inferno and Aaronson, they come together like — '

'Plum and apple,' Jones chipped in. 'Morecambe and Wise,' Kenway suggested. Manson frowned at the levity. The A.C. said. 'You raided the club and found nothing, except marihuana.'

'Kenway was supplied with heroin caps — '

'Not by the club. It took someone to get them.'

Kenway leaned forward and placed a pillbox on the table. 'I got some more last night,' he said. 'They cost me twelve pounds.' The box contained six tablets.

'There you are, then,' the A.C. said. 'What are we waiting for?'

'Faugh!' Manson retorted. He threw up his hands. 'Peddlers, A.C.? We don't want pushers; we want the drug barons, the importers, the suppliers.'

'They are connected with the club somewhere,' Kenway volunteered. 'I'm convinced of that. During the course of every night a dozen or so men and an occasional woman wander up to the door of the manager's office, knock and then go in. When they come out after a few minutes, they go into the toilet. Then they rejoin the club room.'

'Well?' commented the A.C., inviting an explanation.

'When I joined the club the manager, inquiring if I was being looked after said 'if there is anything you want especially, come and see me personally'. He said the same to Asherton. Odd, don't you think? The times I have been to see him personally for something special, I got these.' He pointed to the heroin caps. The A.C. pricked up his ears, metaphorically speaking. 'You think — ?'

'I think the club is a place for satisfying the wants of drug addicts, A.C. I think the people who go to the manager's room get a 'cap', go into the toilet and inject a 'shot' or have a sniff of a powder. Remember what we found in Aaronson's loft — a stub of candle, a needle and heroin caps. Nothing suspicious in that unless you know certain circumstances. The club toilets have separate cubicles, fully enclosed. I could go in, light a candle, prepare a heroin cap, inject a shot with a needle and eyedropper and be back in the club within ten minutes having by then been satisfied by the drug without having any found on me.'

Doctor Manson stared at him with unseeing eyes for a moment or two. He appeared to be visualising something imperceptible to his companions. His brows came together in a narrow line, and his eyes half closed. Then, regarding Kenway thoughtfully, he said: 'How would they convert the caps into liquid for injection?'

★　★　★

Kenway felt in his jacket pocket and produced an envelope. From it he took a small circular object and placed it on the table in front of the Doctor. 'With that,' he said.

Doctor Manson picked it up. It was a metal seal of a soda water bottle which had been prised off with a bottle-opener. The inside between the spread points was stained with a substance sticky to the touch; the outside surface was blackened with a flame deposit. 'I picked it up last night in one of the cubicles,' Kenway explained. 'It had rolled behind the lavatory pan. I'll lay a pound to a penny the Lab. will find evidence of heroin in it.'

Doctor Manson nodded. 'Go on, Kenway,' he said.

'Right. An injection of heroin is made like Aaronson made it, and hey presto, nothing on the addict except an eyedropper in a bottle which may or may not contain eye lotion. You could search him and come away with nothing — which we did, in the raid. Of course, if you are just a 'sniffer' you get enough for that and use it all up.'

'You suggest, Inspector, that the drug is held in the club?' asked the A.C.

'Not in the way you are thinking of, sir.

I think the manager, or somebody, has a very good idea of the number of clients he is likely to receive each night. The most we have noticed going into the manager's office each night is a dozen. Twelve caps of the size we have here could be carried in a matchbox or cigarette case or a carton. Should a customer demand a larger supply, then it takes an hour to get it — as it did for me.'

* * *

'That was good work, Kenway,' Doctor Manson said. The conference over, the Homicide Squad leaders were back in the Doctor's room on the top floor of the Yard. 'It was good observation and initiative.'

'Do you think it a good hypothesis, Doctor?'

'Yes and no. I think the club can be a supply centre for addicts in London who can afford to be members at the prices charged for drinks. That it is, if I may use the phrase, a drug retail centre. What I am wondering is whether it may not be a wholesale establishment with a sales pushing campaign? It is pretty difficult to smuggle heroin into this country. Yet, in the space of three years, the number of addicts in Britain has been more than tripled. Do you read the *Lancet?*' Kenway shook his head.

The Doctor rummaged in a drawer and extracted a cutting. 'Listen to this,' he said, and read: ' 'Known number of drug addicts in Britain numbered 359 in 1957, and this number we estimate to have grown to round about 1,000 (the cutting is dated this year, 1967). This figure, however, is probably too small by half.' The drugs referred to are heroin, morphine and cocaine. Add to the 1,500 Addicts Anonymous, who supplied the figures, the number of addicts not known to that body and you get an appalling amount of heroin circulating throughout the country.'

'All injected or sniffed?' Jones asked.

'No. The latest craze according to the *Lancet* is drug cocktails made by mixing heroin and cocaine or morphine and pethedrine with well-known soft drinks or aperitifs. And we do not know how much of this is being drunk by people who are not addicts in the strict sense of the word. So there are big supplies somewhere — and we do not know whence they come.'

'Robbery and raids on chemists' shops and drug houses,' Jones suggested.

'Peanuts, Fat Man. Both only keep sufficient for medical purposes — the drug houses to supply medical requirements to chemists, and laboratories, and the chemists to dispense prescriptions. The current price of heroin is about two hundred pounds an ounce.'

'You say addicts, Doctor,' Jones interrupted. 'Suppose a cove starts on heroin, how long before he is what they call 'hooked'?'

'Within a month he will acquire a craving for it.'

Kenway, who had lapsed into thought, came up again. 'I don't like to say it, Doctor, but I think the girl Margaret knows something of what goes on. I'm running her down to Brighton for the day tomorrow. It's her night off. We'll go back to her flat and spend the evening there.

I've made good friends with her. I may be able to learn something about the club which can't be acquired by just visiting it.'

The intercom buzzed. The Doctor pressed a lever and the voice from the other end came loud and clear: 'Lab. here, Doctor. That bottle-top you sent over . . . the inside staining under Frohds' reagent gave a brilliant crimson-purple, soon fading. Confirmatory tests with Marquis reagent gave a plain crimson soon fading. I make it diacetylmorphine. Agreed? The outside surface was smoked. Tests on the soot deposit suggest petrol — possibly a lighter. End.'

'Thanks!' Doctor Manson released the lever. 'You heard that, Kenway? Your assumption was correct.'

23

The Narcotics Bureau of New York State were singing loud and long with sarcastic emphasis on the inability of the Customs people to track drug imports, except by the fortunate chance of accident. It wasn't exactly the forty-five pounds of heroin which worried them; that had been obtained and would not, in consequence, go to the drug barons. What was exercising their minds was the fact that Grudelberger had been receiving imports from Abrahams and Company over months, and it was odds of a hundred to one on that most of the imports had contained concealed heroin. Forty-five pounds in one batch was a pretty powerful import, but how many other forty-five pounds had come in earlier — and gone to the black market and been supplied to the 50,000 known addicts in the U.S.A.?

They wanted action by the police and it

wasn't any good going to Interpol, who were bound hand and foot by political considerations. If it came to the point of pulling to pieces every cargo imported from England, the port authorities would be held up like a massive road-block. New York Police, they insisted, had better get busy at the business end — in England. Nobody had thought of heroin coming in from there, it bore, and always had done, an Eastern tang.

The police went back to Grudelberger. That wasn't much use, either. They used every device they knew, including, as a last resort, a lie detector and hypnotism. He knew nothing, he affirmed vehemently, beyond what he had already told them. The imports, he insisted, had been consigned to him as an importing agent. He collected them, drove them to his premises — which were all open and above board. There, they were collected by people who showed him authority to receive them, or were sold by him to customers who inquired for that type of wares, details of which he sent out to the trade in the usual sales propaganda.

'What authority did these customers show?' the police demanded; and received the reply: 'Letters stating that so and so goods had been sent by so and so ship and should arrive on this or that date.' He checked the letters with the cargo assigned to him as agent, and if satisfied allowed the goods to be taken away.

It was an impossible story and the police did not believe one word of it, but there was nothing they could do to disprove it. Grudelberger was, however, held on a charge of being in possession, knowingly or unknowingly, of heroin, since the cases had been addressed to and collected by him. The American law has no truck with the ludicrous idea in Britain that a man is innocent until he is proved guilty; in the U.S.A. it is assumed, logically, that a man wouldn't be arrested unless the police had evidence suggesting his guilt and it was up to him to prove that they hadn't!

Grudelberger, they were quite certain, knew all about the heroin imports. After all in many cases he had to order the goods; nobody in the world of commerce sent goods to an importing agent on chance, or spec. While it is a proved axiom that one has to speculate in order to accumulate, one has to have some guarantee that the speculating has a sporting odds chance of proving accumulative. Fortune, like Lady Luck, may be blind, but not so blind as all that.

So the police under the lash of the Narcotics Bureau, switched their researches from the receiving end to the producing beginning. A Chief of Detectives, of the New York Police, accompanied by an executive officer of the Narcotics Bureau, sailed for England with a formidable dossier on the operations of Grudelberger of New York and A. Abrahams and Company, Limited, of Rotherhithe, London. It contained a list of all the firms who had entrusted cargoes to importer Grudelberger over the past twelve months, together with the nature of the cargoes.

They landed on the Commissioner for the Metropolitan Police in New Scotland Yard without warning or introduction, were received warmly with the request in what way the Commissioner could be of service to his American colleagues. They told him in outline and the Commissioner shot up in his chair, looked like a startled faun and was no longer warm in his reception. 'This is incredible,' he said, and like Pilate of old washed his hands of it. 'I think,' he opined, 'you had better see the head of our Criminal Investigation Department. I am merely the sovereign head of police organisation, you know.'

He pushed them with an introduction to the Assistant Commissioner (Crime): 'Sir Edward . . . Chief O'Brien, Detective Division, New York, and Mr. Oswald Derringer of the Narcotics Division of the same city. Sir Edward Allen, G.C.V.O. They are here, A.C., with a story which is very disturbing.'

'That,' Chief O'Brien said, 'is the understatement of the year. Say, you listen to this.'

Sir Edward listened, fingering his cravat above a lavender vest which matched his black coat and striped trousers, and placing and replacing a rimless monocle in his perfectly good left eye — an operation which appeared to have a stunning effect on the narcotics representative — he stared as though he himself was under the influence of a narcotic drug. The A.C. did not, in fact, listen for long, for he broke into the recital.

'It is rather a coincidence, Chief, that we are ourselves involved at the moment in a very intricate drug problem which also centres on heroin. I would like you to come along with me to meet Commander Doctor Harry Manson, head of our Forensic Department. It is he who is concerned with the case I have mentioned, and murder is mixed up in it.'

So, in Doctor Manson's study with Superintendent Jones and Chief Inspector Kenway also present, the story of the ship *Invista* and its cargo was told in full, in the American idiom and accent, which is almost parallel to speaking in a foreign language. Then the Chief relit his foul-smelling ten-cent cigar, looped his fingers in the armholes of his waistcoat, looked round and said: 'Waal, whadjer say to that?'

'You apparently hold the opinion,

Chief, that other consignments sent through Grudelberger may also have contained concealed heroin?' the Doctor asked.

'Yew kin say that again, sir — and how.'

'And you have no idea of the identity of the persons to whom those goods were ultimately delivered?'

'No, siree. Grudelberger says they showed a letter of notification that the goods had been sent — and that's all.'

'But the letters must bear a signature.'

'Sure they gotta name, like your English John Doe. You get lookin' round in London for John Doe. Boy, the gangs who handle dope in our burg have as many names as there are in the telephone directory.'

'The letters from this Abrahams and Company — they were signed?'

'Sure. Grudelberger couldn't remember the name, but after we worked him over a bit his memory sorta returned and he said the guy signing about the pottery was name of Maddison.'

A half-strangled exclamation came from Kenway. Doctor Manson turned towards him. 'Something?' he asked.

'Possibly, Doctor. Do you recall Mitchell telling us of three men in the Inferno who always sit at the same table together? One of them was compromised in a raid on a youth club. Well, I've heard the name Maddison called to one of them.'

'You know him?' the Chief asked.

'We think we know *of* him. He's under suspicion of being concerned in the peddling of drugs, but so far it is only suspicion.'

'Waal, you've got sumpin on him now.'

The American deputation rose and left. 'We'll be staying at your Savoy,' the Chief announced, 'until we get the lowdown on how the dope is gett'n' on board ships to us.'

'Gor blimey,' Jones said when they had gone. 'That's a ruddy nice goin' on. What are we goin' to do about it?'

'Look up Maddison to begin with. Is he in the phone book?'

'Which of them would you like, Doctor?' Kenway asked after some minutes. There's a list of them, all London or suburban addresses.'

'Pay a series of social calls?' from Jones. The Doctor shook his head. 'The only people who can identify him are Mitchell and Kenway, and they are incognito in the Inferno. Get on to the C.I.D. in the districts and get them to make local inquiries.'

'Eliminate 'em, Doctor, eh?' Old Fat Man said, and grinned.

'If we run him down, is he to be picked up?' Kenway put the query.

'No. Tail him for the time being. See where he goes, who he speaks to, everything he does. If he's on the telephone we'll have his number tapped. We'll have to see the Home Secretary for that. Better put two or three men on the tailing, *if* we trace him.'

'If, Doctor? Got any doubts about it?' Jones asked the question.

Doctor Manson looked at him, reflectively. 'People engaged in this are not fools, Fat Man. If they are caught they know it means a stiff sentence. Were you smuggling heroin to America would you sign your name to a letter advising that a cargo was on the way, knowing that if anything went wrong you would be in the net? Or would you pick a name from, say, the London Directory, a name of which there are a reasonable number, like Jones, Smith — or Maddison?'

24

The morrow's outing was not so much a day's trip to Brighton as a safari into the Rapes of Sussex. Margaret revealed that it was years since she had seen any country more than that represented by the greenswards of London parks; and as for farm animals she had seen by accident sheep in Hyde Park being chased by a dog: which was a libellous description of the well-known Sheep Dog Trials in that rendezvous. Kenway in his guise as Emerson accordingly took what may be described as the garden route to the seaside resort beginning, in effect, after they had shaken their heels off Horley.

A bit of an enthusiast on archaeology and history the safari was enlivened by him with a descriptive commentary on the scenery slipping past them. A detour along a lane some half a mile beyond the Surrey town of Horley halted for a few moments at what was obviously the remains of a moat, and nothing else. 'Once,' Kenway said, 'King Alfred the Great built a wooden fortress near here, with a deep moat filled with water surrounding it. He called it Danresfeld, and it formed a bequest in his will. It became known as Thunderfeld Castle. Alfred died in 901, so this moat is more than a thousand years old. Isn't that wonderful to think of? Let's have a drink here.'

A few miles further along and the car turned into Tinsley Green. Kenway pulled up in front of the Greyhound Inn — and chuckled. 'When I was a boy I used to come to play marbles here on Good Friday morning.'

'Play marbles?' Margaret echoed.

'Sure. Marbles. It's a kind of tradition here on Good Friday. There are ranks of marble players trying to win the British Individual Marbles Championship. They've been playing marbles here on Good Friday since the days of Queen Elizabeth — the first one, I mean.'

The next few miles passed in silence, Margaret revelling in the countryside, the green fields, the little hamlets until the car ran into a township. 'Where's this?' she asked.

'East Grinstead. Look at it as we go through.' Clear of the streets, he pulled into the side of the country road which stretched ahead. 'I'll tell you a story, Margaret. Nearly a thousand years ago all this part of the country was an enormous forest called Andredesweald. It had been so for hundreds of years. Then one day people arrived here, cut down some trees and made a clearing so that they could build homes. With the trees gone, the sunlight penetrated, and grass grew where there had been only bracken before. So people called the clearing Grenested, which means a green place. When another clearing was made many years later people distinguished between the two by calling one place East Grinstead and the other West Grinstead.'

'Cor,' Margaret said. 'Just think of people living here all that while ago.' Kenway grinned. Like most young people of today she had never heard of Londinium, in which their ancestors had lived more than two thousand years ago: and she walking in their footsteps every day of her life.

A few miles further on they ran into the heart of South Downs country, that verdant paradise rolling high and low, whose green fields were raided by the Belgae and for generations afterwards saw war from the Saxons, from Offa King of Mercia, from the Danes and last of all from William the Bastard, called The Conqueror. Kings of Wessex came and went. Blood nurtured its soil and raised crops of corn and animals. Through Ditchling with its towering beacon Kenway drove to Clayton and pulled up at the church.

'Come in, Margaret,' he said. 'I want to show you something.' They entered the church. 'Look,' he said. On the nave and chancel walls were frescoes. 'They're wonderful, Reggie,' Margaret said. 'What are they and who did them?'

'The Last Judgement . . . and a monk. Nine hundred years ago this church belonged to a Benedictine monastery at Lewes. A monk came from there and spent years in here painting the frescoes. They're famous, by the way.'

They re-entered the car and a short run by way of Pyecombe landed them in Brighton. They found a vacant space in the car park at the back of the coastal road. 'I'm hungry. Lunch first,' Kenway announced. He was in a bit of a dilemma. He did not want to meet any police officer who knew him — and quite a few did — and who might come up with a welcome to the chief inspector. Accordingly, the popular lunching houses were closed to them; instead, he wound a roundabout way which led through narrow lanes, almost like entries, into the Market Place, where there stood a small Regency-style restaurant. They lunched off a Lucullus-like menu, helped by a bottle of table wine.

Brighton still lives on 'Prinny' the Prince Regent and Dr. Russell. The pair together put the town on the map, the Prince as a place of residence, and the doctor as a health resort. Together Kenway and Margaret toured the Prince's fantastic Chinese nightmare building called The Pavilion, the beautiful Regency squares and buildings and the elegant terraces. In the Steyne while on a short cut to the beach, Margaret paused to read a plaque on a building. Mrs. FitzHerbert, it said, had lived there. 'Ah, I know all about her,' she said. 'The Prince's fancy woman.'

'Wrong, Margaret,' Kenway corrected. 'She was not his mistress, but a woman very badly wronged by her husband — and her husband was the Prince. They were married secretly and morganatically. If anyone was his mistress, apart from the acknowledged ones, then it was Queen Caroline, because Mrs. FitzHerbert had been his wife ten years before he married Caroline and made her queen of England.'

'Then why didn't Mrs. FitzHerbert become queen?'

'Because in those days the wife of a royal person, and especially of the heir to the throne had of necessity herself to be of royal blood. We've changed to common sense and democracy today.' The remainder of the day was spent lazing on the beach and they finally reached London by nine o'clock, going straight to Margaret's flat in Maida Vale. Seated on a settee and balancing a cup of tea Margaret said: 'I *have* enjoyed today, Reggie. Thank you very much. I feel wonderful.'

'That's Doctor Brighton's doing.'

'Funny. Hookey always calls it Doctor Brighton. Why doctor?'

'Due to a doctor named Russell who lived there. He proclaimed that sea bathing and drinking sea water could alleviate or cure physical ailments, and Brighton was the first to popularise sea-bathing by providing bathing huts on wheels which were trundled down the sands to the water's edge. In point of fact there is something in the 'doctor' idea because the air in Brighton is said to be as good as that of Davos in Switzerland, for consumptives.'

So far the day had passed without any reference to the Inferno Club, its members, and Margaret's job there. Kenway now endeavoured to extract what information he could which could link up the club with the three murders he,

Doctor Manson and Jones were investigating. He prepared for it with shock tactics. Taking a snuff-box from a waistcoat pocket he flipped open the lid and extracted between thumb and forefinger a pinch of white powder which he proceeded to sniff up his nostrils. Margaret, watching him, cried out in distress: 'No,' she said. 'Oh my God, I thought you were different and loved you for it. Now, you're just like all the others — just come to the club for kicks.' She appeared to be on the verge of tears.

'This?' Kenway said and glanced at the snuff-box. 'Oh, don't be scared, Margaret. There's nothing to it. I just take a sniff now and then when I'm tired. Bucks me up no end. I stop when I want to. I'm not likely to become an addict, you know.'

'No? The usual story; that's just what Mr. Aaronson said.'

'Aaronson? Do you mean he became hooked?'

'Of course he became hooked. He used to go into mad moods. Began to dance like a ballet dancer all round the club and once he tried to fight a lion which he said was chasing him across the desert. They had to overpower him and get him out. Next night he was as quiet as you please.'

'Funny. He seemed all right the times I saw him. It's an odd thing he's never appeared to see if I joined the club. I certainly expected to meet him. Wonder what the devil's happened to him. What did he do for a living?'

'I don't know,' she said. She shook her head so violently that her long hair swung from side to side. 'He never replied when asked. We never knew much about him at all. You see, we only saw him at night in the club.'

'Never met him during the day, like me?'

'No. I liked him a lot and tried to get him to take me to Kew or Richmond but he always said he couldn't manage it. I don't think he was very well off because he was poorly dressed, really.'

'Very funny. Where does he live? I might go round and see if he's all right.'

'I don't know. If anybody knows it's Hookey. They were close friends. Only

208

Hookey doesn't seem to worry about him any more.'

Kenway stood up. 'Coo, Margaret, it's warm in here,' he said, and slipped off his jacket. Sitting by her side on the settee he hitched up his shirt cuffs. 'You know, Reggie, this is lovely — ' Her voice ceased suddenly and bending forward she pushed up his shirt sleeve. For a second she stared at the bare forearm thus presented. 'Is this why you keep going into the office, Reggie?' she asked, and pointed. Two, small, red punctures were visible on the outside of Kenway's forearm.

He put on a very creditable look of dismay. 'Look, Margaret — every time I go into the office? I've only been in twice.'

'And had a shot each time?'

'Good Lord, no. I only wanted to see what it felt like. Don't worry, girl. It made me feel so awful that I never want to experience it again.'

'And sniffing?'

'Yes, and sniffing. Look.' He rose, walked her into the kitchen and emptied the contents of the snuff-box down the sink. 'There.'

'Good lad,' she said and smiled. 'Now look, Reggie. Don't come to the club any more. I'd like to see you and have days like this again. You know this address and you can have my phone number. Contact me here at any time during the morning, but keep away from the club.'

Kenway pondered over his answer. He was in a quandary, and knew it. His investigations were making progress but had not, as yet, provided any conclusions on which the Yard could take any action to link his investigations with murder. He *had* to continue with the club, but at the same time placate his companion.

'Look, Margaret,' he said at last. 'I don't want to do that. I like the company, I like the music and the atmosphere. I don't know much of London and when I come here from Manchester I enjoy the time spent in the Inferno. But I promise you — no more sniffing and no more shots.'

He paused, considering his next move. He had, he felt, and was rather ashamed of it, induced a mood in Margaret when she might be persuaded to let out information about the club without her suspicions being aroused. It surprised him that, being part of the club's staff, she should be shocked and disturbed at the fact that he had been indulging in heroin. 'Look,' he said. 'When you saw me sniffing just now you said I was the same as all the others, using the club to get kicks. Do you mean that all the members go there for kicks?'

'No, not all. But I should say half are addicts, or on the way to becoming so. You can pick them out by seeing them go into Petersen's office.'

'You mean they get the stuff there?'

'I should say so. You ought to know. You got it there yourself, didn't you?'

'But when the club was raided — a complete surprise — nothing was found. How do you account for that?'

'I know. I thought they were booked when the police piled in. But nothing happened except that a few members were fined.'

'Who owns the Inferno?'

'That's the 64-dollar question, Reggie. Everybody would like to know.'

'The manager? He holds the licence?'

'Petersen? No. He's nothing really. Hookey has far more authority than Petersen. If Hookey says no, and Petersen says yes — then it's 'No'. They quarrel about things, but Hookey always wins.'

'Hookey the owner?'

'No. I don't think so.'

'You know, Margaret, knowing what you do and not agreeing with dope, I wonder you work there. Why do you?'

'Blame my parents, Reggie.' She made a moue. 'I was sent to a good school, then to a finishing school where I learned deportment and how to be a great hostess, how to dress, behave in a social set — and that's all. When mother and father died we found they had lost a fortune in bad investments; I think they got into the hands of a crook company. I had no training in anything by which I could earn a living. You tell me where, outside the Inferno, I could earn more than twenty pounds a week with commission that is, and thus keep up this flat. Sure, I know and suspect what goes on in the club, but if men are such fools as to degrade and ruin themselves what can I do about it? Am I my brother's keeper? Now, you'd better be going. It's late and I'm tired after a perfectly marvellous day.'

In bed that night Margaret patted herself on the back at having weaned Emerson from the drug habit. It was not until very much later that she learned that the snuff-box had contained only talcum powder, and that the puncture marks on his forearm had been deliberately made with a hypodermic syringe with the idea of letting her see them, and draw conclusions. By that time the triple murders and the tale of drugs had become a thing of the past.

25

Doctor Manson heard next morning Kenway's account of the Inferno Club as told him by the girl. It included the friendship that had existed between the mysterious and vanished Aaronson and Hookey, the club's bandleader and heroin addict. 'The girl indicated, I gather, that Aaronson became an addict through the club,' the Doctor said. 'That rather supports what we found in Water Street. But that dancing like a wild dervish and chasing lions which did not exist in a desert that wasn't there — that isn't heroin aftermath, and not even caused by lack of heroin in an addict. It sounds to me more like a 'trip' with LSD. The fact that a 'trip' extends in effect to roughly twenty-four hours at a minimum and that the following night Aaronson was normal is indicative of the drug.'

'What I can't understand, Doctor, is the disappearance of Aaronson. He used

214

to live in the club practically every night. Hookey was his familiar and now has no interest in him or his whereabouts. And Aaronson, you remember, we thought was the man dead in Water Street.'

The Doctor eyed him. There was on his face a Sphinxlike blankness. He thought for a moment before he spoke. 'Are you suggesting, Kenway, that Hookey shows no interest in the man because there is no longer any reason for interest?'

'Something like that — yes.'

'That the body in Water Street is believed by Hookey to have been that of Aaronson?'

'Yes. We've never given it a name — only the body of an unidentified man.'

The Doctor's eyes relaxed. 'That is in my mind, too. I think we shall have to take a closer interest in the Inferno — '

'Leave it for a few days, Doctor. I've an idea I'd like to try out which may produce some information. I'd rather not disclose it for the moment.'

'Go your ways,' Manson said with a smile.

'Good. How did the Fat Man progress

with our American cousins' moaning?'

'Frustrating . . . blank . . . and very odd.'

★ ★ ★

Frustrating was the word for it. Jones grumbling (as usual) at being switched off direct homicide to investigate something which, according to the Doctor, was merely tied up with homicide, commenced his task by looking through the telephone directory for the number of A. Abrahams and Co. There was not, he found, any listed number. He called up the central exchange. 'Scotland Yard,' he roared through the mouthpiece nearly blasting the ears off the girl at the other end. 'I want the ex-directory number of A. Abrahams and Company, Limited, Liverpool Street, Rotherhithe.'

'Hold the line,' the voice said. 'I'll look it up. Who is inquiring?'

'Chief Superintendent Jones, Central Office.'

Three minutes passed permeated by mutterings from the Fat Man which sounded like the rumblings of a volcano about to erupt. Then: 'Sorry, Superintendent. We have no ex-directory number for A. Abrahams and Co. Ltd. In fact there isn't a telephone rented in that name.'

'Cor stone the flaming crows,' Jones exploded, banged his bowler hat on his head and waddled his eighteen stone into City Road. He showed his warrant card. 'Want to see registration of A. Abrahams and Co., Ltd., exporting agency, Liverpool Street, Rotherhithe,' he announced. 'Directors' names, annual report . . . pronto.'

'Take a seat, Super.' He did so. A quarter of an hour passed, then the clerk returned and beckoned him forward. 'There isn't any such company, Super,' he said. Jones's face went nearly purple. His patience was, to use a cliché, nearly exhausted. He leaned over the desk, grabbed the clerk by a lapel and pushed his face against that of the unfortunate man. 'Look, son,' he said. 'They've been exporting goods by ship to America. I gotta copy of their billhead. A fortnight ago three bloody great cases of pottery

217

were taken off'n ship in New York harbour. They had been sent, according to a bill of lading by this 'ere A.Abrahams and Company. Who d'ye reckon loaded the pottery? A flaming fairy?' The last sentence came in a Jones roar and caused a fluttering among customers. 'Now you go and get me the details of this 'ere firm.'

The clerk released his lapel from Jones's grip. 'Now see here, Super,' he said. 'We are employed by the Government — right? When you form a company, it has to be registered — right? When it's registered, you have to pay a fee. Each year you have to send in the company's annual return and you have to pay an annual registration fee else we're after you for it. Now, did you ever hear of any government department letting any taxpayer off paying his just dues — ?'

'No, the ruddy robbers take more than their just dues,' Jones broke in.

'Well, there you are, then. We don't let anybody jib us. No fees have been received by us from any company of the name and address you mentioned. I looked that up, too, in case the registration had been mislaid in the company files. *Quod erat demonstrandum*, there ain't no such company.'

★   ★   ★

'Damn and blast to blazes,' Jones said to Doctor Manson reporting on the failure. ''E said sumptin about quoding and demonstrating. What's that gotta do with it?'

Manson chuckled. 'He was throwing Latin in your face, Fat Man. He meant that the facts he had given you proved that the company had no existence. You had better hop down — ' he chuckled a little at the idea of Old Fat Man's eighteen stone hopping anywhere 'to the address of this mythical company and see what it is all about. Take Barratt with you.'

Detective Sergeant Barratt, the Doctor's secretary, was in the Homicide General Office. 'We gotta slog down to this dive,' Jones said after explaining the débâcle in City Road. 'Be the death o' me, this detectin',' he moaned.

'So! It's kept you alive and kicking and eating damned near fifty years, you old fraud. C'mon.'

No Squad car was available so they went by bus, wandering through traffic and innumerable bus stops to the High Street, and from there took to their feet into Liverpool Street. It was a short and unsavoury thoroughfare. They traversed the full length on either side without seeing any premises marked Abrahams and Co.; there was not, in fact, any premises at all that looked like housing a company of any kind, let alone one doing an export trade in heavy goods.

Jones was perspiring freely from the warm day and the walking. They came to a public house. 'We'll go in and have a freshener,' he said.

'No, you don't, you old fraud. Let's find the company first,' Barratt insisted. They passed, Jones gazing back at the pub entrance with the lugubrious passion of Orpheus surveying Eurydice at Hell's Mouth.

'Suppose there isn't another Liverpool

Street, is there?' Barratt asked. 'There is,' Jones retorted. 'But it ain't in Rotherhithe. It's the one with the dirty bloody station and the worst trains.'

'Well, I can't see any warehouses in this one. Was there a number given?'

'Lumme,' Jones said. 'Fancy me forgettin' that. Was lookin' for a warehouse. Number 27 according to the Yanks.'

'Glory be,' said Barratt. 'Here it is. Crumbs!' He stared. Jones stared. Number 27 was a small and very dirty general shop, the windows of which contained a collection of fly-blown tins of soup, meats, etc., with a side window covered with written advertisements for things wanted or for sale. They went in. A decrepit specimen of humanity greeted them.

'You Abrahams and Co.?' Jones demanded. The old man eyed them for a fraction of a minute, then tottered round the counter to the door. He beckoned them and they followed into the street. Pointing to the board above the shop front he spluttered: 'I suppose you can read, can't you?' The board bore in lettering almost obliterated by age the inscription, 'Samuel Isaacs, Grocery.'

Jones hustled him back in the shop and pinned him against the counter with his bulk. 'Isaacs, is it?' he bellowed. 'Then how comes it that letters are sent from this address in the name of Abrahams and Company?'

'That's my business. What in hell has it to do with you?'

Old Fat Man produced his warrant card and pushed it under the old man's eyes. 'It's got this to do with me, son, so open up, or I'll have you in the clink afore you can say Jehovah.'

'They 'as letters sent here, Mister.'

'An' 'ave the address printed on their notepaper, too. When you gets letters where do you send 'em?'

'I don't.'

'C'mon Barratt,' Jones said. 'Let's get him up to Central and beat it out'a him.' He moved to take Isaacs.

'All right,' Isaacs surrendered. 'A g . . . g . . . ent c-calls for 'em.'

'An' whom might this gent be, eh?'

'Dunno.' Jones made a move forward

and the Jew said: 'Name o' Maddison, guv'nor.'

'Calls regularly does he?'

'Nah. Only when he's expecting a letter.'

'When did he last call?'

'It'd be about three weeks or a month ago.'

'How long have you been taking in letters for Abrahams?'

'About eight months. He gives me seven and a kick for each letter.'

'He does, does he? Usual price for accommodation letters is about five bob a week, and you get seven and a kick for each letter. You in this racket, or something?'

'I allus thought it were a bit funny. But the money's useful down here. Look at the bloody shop.'

'What kind of cove is this man Maddison?'

'Livin' spit of him (pointing to Barratt). Might be him.'

'What!'

Jones turned towards the sergeant, portentously. 'Is it you?' he asked.

'Is it? Why you flat bladder of lard!'
Jones's left eye closed in a wink. 'About
the same build as the sergeant?'

'Yes, but he got nasty eyes. They
frighten me.'

Jones got hold of his lapel again. 'If he
comes here again for a letter and you
don't let the cops know *I'll* frighten you
out'a your ruddy skin. If a letter comes,
you let the cop house know, pronto. An' if
you mentions a word of all this you're in
for a stretch,' which wasn't true, but
Isaacs could be scared stiff that it might
be possible.

'He'd murder me if he know'd I'd told
you anything,' Isaacs protested. Jones
pushed his face close to the old man's
and he scowled: 'Son,' he said, 'there's
things that can be done worse then
murder. *An' I knows all about* 'em and
how to do 'em. See.'

They left the shop. As he went through
the door Jones turned and looked at
Isaacs, by now half terrified.

'*Remember*,' he said.

That was the story that they brought
back to Doctor Manson, and the story

that the Doctor told in précis to Kenway. It had by then been retailed to the American delegation. 'Oh Lord, an accommodation address,' Kenway said. 'That's a new one on me for a company. Anyhow the visit was a bit of luck. We know Maddison — in the Inferno.'

'We know nothing of the sort,' the Doctor informed him. 'The man you and Asherton described is an Angus Robertson, in the tobacco trade. We've had Asherton investigate him. He lives in Harrow Weald and has been, and is being, watched by the police for some time on suspicion of being concerned in hi-jacking cigarette cargoes.'

'But, Doctor, we definitely heard the name Maddison mentioned. I'll see what I can find out about that from Margaret.'

26

A conference was held in the room of the Commissioner of the Metropolitan Police. Present were the Commissioner, the Assistant Commissioner (Crime), Chief Inspector Wellbeing, head of the Narcotics Squad, Superintendent Johns, senior executive officer of Customs and Excise, his deputy, and Doctor Manson. A request from the Chief of Detectives of New York that he should sit in had been turned down. It was a matter for the British police he was told, acting on information given them. The British police would do their own work, thank you, free from outside help or influence.

The topic?

Heroin.

Not just the heroin seized through the circumstance of accident in New York harbour. The effective persuasions on Grudelberger had disclosed that he had on three occasions received merchandise consigned by Abrahams and Co., and had delivered them, or rather handed them over, to importers he didn't know but who had produced the necessary authority. It was pretty obvious from Jones's visit to Rotherhithe that there was no such firm. It followed, therefore, that the firm was an invention of a gang or other association and the merchandise shipped was merely a disguise for hidden cargo, and that hidden cargo was certainly drugs, and in all probability heroin and its allied drugs, morphine and pethedrine. The value of the drugs was immeasurably greater in the U.S.A. than in Britain or anywhere in Europe. According to the U.S.A. Narcotics Squad, the value in the New York black market of the drug seized on the *Invista* was £700,000. The price of heroin in Britain was about £200 an ounce which would amount to approximately £144,000 for the amount seized in New York.

It was unlikely that the earlier imports had contained an equal quantity of the drug; Grudelberger had stated that each had consisted of a single case of goods.

The operators, encouraged by success, had become greedy. But at a conservative estimate some three-quarters of a million pounds worth of heroin and associated drugs had been smuggled from Britain into the U.S.A.

In order to export it it had first to be acquired. 'Where from?' the Commissioner inquired, and looked across at Doctor Manson. The Doctor waved a hand in the direction of Inspector Wellbeing. 'Don't look at me, Commissioner,' he said. 'I'm homicide and my interest in these proceedings is who killed three men. Drugs appear to be mixed up in it, but I'm not concerned with drug importations or exports.'

'I can't answer you,' Wellbeing admitted. 'There are several ways in which heroin and morphine can be obtained. Legitimately, it can be purchased. Laboratories use it for experimental purposes, drug houses buy it for inclusion in medicines, mostly cough and bronchial preparations, chemists keep supplies for the dispensing of medical prescriptions. Thus, purchase is possible . . . '

'On a commercial basis?' the A.C. asked.

'If smuggled into the U.S.A. with that country's load of addicts — certainly, sir. Illegitimately, it can be obtained through raids on drug factories, on medical associations and chemists premises and by hi-jacking operations.'

'And by smuggling?' the A.C. asked.

'I'll come to that later. Now, every raid on premises such as I have enumerated is reported to the police — you know that. Hi-jacking is also reported to the police. Laboratories have to provide returns of all scheduled drugs they distil and process; drug houses the same. Chemists must show their purchases and sales, and like doctors must keep a register. So do hospitals. There is thus a complete check on scheduled drugs, particularly heroin, morphine and opium.'

Doctor Manson nodded. 'And what are we to gather from all that?' he asked.

Inspector Wellbeing leaned forward, elbows on the large oval-shaped and polished desk. He thrust his head belligerently forward and pointed a finger at the company. 'It means this,' he said, 'that we have a pretty reliable knowledge of what heroin there is here. It means, gentlemen, that *there never was three-quarters of a million pounds' worth of heroin available to anyone in this country to sell — either by purchase or by theft.*'

The shocked silence that followed the announcement could almost be felt so loaded was the atmosphere. It lasted for the space of half a minute — which is a long time for silence. The Commissioner relieved the situation. 'But, good heavens, Chief, it *was* exported. We know that forty-five pounds were seized from a cargo sent from here. Damn it, the American narcotics people testify to that effect. The dock people saw it. You aren't suggesting they are lying, are you?'

'No, sir — of course not. They wouldn't have come here unless they were on sure and certain ground. All I am saying is *what I know to be the case.*'

There followed a second protracted silence. In five minds was but a single thought, five pairs of eyes looked everywhere except at the owner of the sixth pair. The Commissioner coughed, awkwardly. Then Superintendent Johns spoke:

'If I interpret the Chief Inspector correctly that there was never that supply in the country legitimately, then I can only conclude that he holds the view that it came here illegitimately.'

The Chief Inspector nodded.

'Smuggled?' The Commissioner looked across at the Narcotics chief. 'That is so,' Wellbeing agreed.

'Then I deny it — most emphatically.' Superintendent Johns spoke with considerable heat that brought an angry colour to his face. 'It's fantastic . . . absolutely fantastic. All my men are experts at detecting such imports. I don't deny that now and then small packets of heroin are smuggled in — and found. During the past twelve months we have uncovered thirty or forty instances of drugs. We have unearthed them in hand luggage, in baggage, in car axle boxes, in the soles of shoes, in buoys dropped as moorings by yachts, in all kinds of hiding places in ships interiors. We have even discovered a quantity in a consignment of broom handles from Germany. We sawed the handles in half and found parts of them hollowed out. We've unearthed morphine in artificial flowers packed in the south of France . . . '

'Then why is it fantastic the idea that quantities should slip into the country?' the Commissioner asked.

'I have been referring to small amounts, sir. Now, loose heroin in quantity has, like raw opium, a distinctive smell. Not so penetrating as opium, but still detectable. No bulk could get past us, not even when diluted with lactose or milk sugar, which is to heroin what brandy is to wine. Amounts such as have been mentioned in connection with this inquiry would be impossible to get past us.'

'Well,' the Commissioner wound up, 'the stuff was sent from here and must, accordingly have been here first. Narcotics had better get busy and find out how. We've closed the Abrahams end, but it isn't likely that that will be the end of the traffic.'

They *had* closed the Abrahams end. Detectives searching for clues to the fraudulent firm or for the man who had collected the letters failed to find any traces. Grudelberger had stated that he received intimation of the despatch of goods on the notepaper of A. Abrahams and Co., Ltd. This appeared the most likely pointer for detectives. Printers over a wide area were circularised and visited, but none had any record of printing such noteheads. Then, the goods must have been taken to London docks in some sort of conveyance. The crates landed in New York would have necessitated a van of considerable size and weight. Yet, carriers of goods had had no orders for such a journey; nor had various firms who hired out vans by the journey, day or week. At the London docks the three crates were recorded as having been received for shipping, but as to how they had been transported there the dock people had no idea. It wasn't their business to inquire into transport, they pointed out.

Observation that had been kept on the

Liverpool Street shop was now with-drawn; it was obvious that Abrahams and Company would know that something had gone wrong; in consequence they would give the shop a wide berth.

Doctor Manson caught up with Inspector Wellbeing on the staircase after the conference with the Commissioner had ended. 'I was going to give you a ring, Doctor,' the inspector said. 'I'd like to have a talk with you — and some advice.' In the laboratory study he unburdened himself. 'You said at the conference, Doctor, that you are interested only in homicide and you explained that drugs seemed to be mixed up with homicide. What did you mean by that?'

He listened to the story of the shooting of Barstowe in the Dilettantes' Club, the death of the unidentified man in Water Street, of the stabbing of the Slasher, the mystery of Aaronson; the curious finds in the Water Street hovel, and the riddle presented by Kenway's visits to the Inferno Club.

The inspector nodded slowly. 'You perhaps know that we have suspicions in that connection, apart from your inquiries. A number of known addicts use the club, especially one or two pop groups. You know half the addiction is among the pop groups and their supporters and it is their songs, especially about LSD, that is encouraging their fans to start drugging and smoking marihuana. I wish to God the authorities, especially magistrates, would put them out of the way of temptation.'

'I agree,' Manson said. 'Most emphatically. But never mind; pop and swing which is only a throwback to the lewd nigger songs of the past, is on its way out and the old time and musical ballad is coming back. Regarding heroin, you are certain that the amounts we have been talking about could not have been imported. I appreciate between ourselves that it may be necessary for policy's sake to deny it outright; I have to act that way myself occasionally, lest disclosures should adversely affect investigation.'

'Definitely not, Doctor. I can assure you that it is incredible that such amounts should pass us, or fail to come to our knowledge in the Narcotics Bureau. Besides, we would have heard from the International organisation if such quantities had been bandied around among drug dealers overseas. They have methods which are not allowed here, you know?'

He paused. Then: 'How is heroin obtained, Doctor? I am a detective and qualified to make investigations into the trade, but not a scientist as yourself. I know the simple facts — that is comes from morphine. But how?'

'Well, briefly, heroin is hydrochloride of the diacetyl derivative of morphine, obtained by acting on morphine with acetic anhydride. It produces greater and quicker effects than morphine, and is more habit forming.'

'So you have to have morphine to produce heroin. How is morphine obtained?'

'It's an alkaloid contained in opium. The juice of the opium poppy is solidified by evaporation and comes out in the form of a dark brown or black unequal mass very much like coarse tobacco. Morphine is extracted from this.'

'So the foundation of heroin is opium. Can anyone with the necessary scientific knowledge produce it?'

'Lord, no, Wellbeing. It requires elaborate machinery in a modern laboratory, and so on.' The Doctor hesitated and then went on: 'Were I asked to offer advice, I would suggest that you check all laboratories. I — '

'You think that one could — ?'

'Improbable, but not impossible. Remember the advice of the Oracle of Delphi.'

27

Alitur vitium vivitque tegendo wrote Virgil, and it would not be easy to find anywhere where vice more thrived and lived by concealment than it did in the Inferno Club. But concealment engaged in by any number of persons depends for success on hazard and the peculiar armour of trust among themselves. A wise old Divine named Fuller arrived at the realisation of this when, more than 200 years ago, he devised a proverb that still lives in theory and fact today — 'He who trusteth not is not deceived.'

The club had put a certain amount of trust in their member, Reginald Emerson. He had, they remembered, been arrested during a raid on its premises, fined for having certain drugs in his possession, and had refused to say where he had obtained those drugs. On his return to the club he had been loud in the denunciation of police methods in searching the persons of customers.

Also he was a purchaser through the management of heroin and was obviously (so the management thought) on the way to becoming 'hooked' and would thus, like other addicts, keep secret the source of his supplies lest disaster overtook him in being unable to get the necessary amounts to satisfy his craving. He was particularly friendly with the orchestra conductor, himself an addict, and generally had a glass of champagne with him during an orchestral recess.

Although nothing spectacular had been achieved by his inquiries and those of Asherton (Detective Sergeant Mitchell) they, nevertheless, had produced some results. In the filed reports made by both of them there figured some thirty names of those members who from time to time walked into the manager's office. There was little doubt that the visits were on a line with the invitation to Kenway when he became a member — that if there was anything special (the word was emphasised) he should see him (the manager) personally. Kenway had accepted the invitation and had asked for and obtained heroin 'caps'. So, obviously, had others who visited the room.

They included three Pop groups who entered the club after midnight at the end of their performances elsewhere. Kenway's report on these said that two of the groups featured in their programmes songs with psychedelic suggestions in words. There seemed little doubt, Kenway reported, that there was available through membership supplies of LSD for 'trips' as well as heroin for 'shots'. How and when such supplies became available was a riddle which the raid on the club had failed to solve.

It was on the fourth night following the Yard conference that there occurred an incident which illustrated the words of Fuller the Divine and which was subsequently to lead to a solution of murder, though not before a considerable time had elapsed. Kenway decided to make another appearance in the club. When he entered, Margaret was dancing with a member and was being entertained between dances with champagne. Kenway accordingly took a seat at a vacant table and called for a whisky and soda.

Presently he rose, walked to the manager's office, knocked and entered. The manager and Hookey were seated at a table. 'Oh, sorry. I didn't know you were engaged,' he apologised. 'All right Emerson. Come right in . . . Have a drink. Just back from the North?'

'Actually, no. I've been back a couple of days but I've been busy. I . . . er . . . want . . . a supply.'

'Six?' Petersen asked.

'No, a few more. I've a couple of friends in Manchester who are in a hole. Supplies seem to have run out up there.'

'In Manchester!' Hookey made it sound like an ejaculation of surprise. He looked across at Petersen. 'It could be the solution,' he said reflectively. Kenway turned towards him. 'Solution of what?' he asked.

'When are you going back to Manchester, Emerson?'

'12.40 train from Euston. Why?' He had had to think very quickly.

'It *could* be the answer,' Petersen said.

'Look, Emerson, would you do us a favour?' He lifted a brief-case from a drawer. 'As you are going to Manchester could you take this with you?' The case was of brief size, such as is carried by lawyers, and bore in gold lettering the inscription 'International Entertainments Limited.'

'I could do so easily,' Kenway said. 'Where do I deliver it?'

'What time do you arrive?'

'At 4.35 in the morning.'

'Right. I can arrange for someone to meet the train and relieve you of it. In point of fact you'll be doing us a really good turn.' He held up a pile of sheet music. 'You see, these are band parts and scripts which have to be in Salford before noon tomorrow, or a show won't be able to open. We only learned by telephone half an hour ago that the parts sent three days ago have not arrived. We can't get these replacements there by post in time, and we've been looking round for a messenger, but candidly we haven't a man we can trust.'

'I'll take it with pleasure. I'll have to

leave here fairly early to settle up for my room.'

'That suits us. There are one or two revisions in the stuff we'll have to make. Let's see . . . ' He ruminated for a few moments. 'Do you know the all-night restaurant opposite the station across the road?' Kenway nodded. 'If you sit at the double table just inside the entrance, one of the club staff, or myself, will bring you the case.'

'My caps?' Kenway asked.

'Oh yes. You aren't going away for an hour, are you? We'll rout some up for you by then.' Kenway took out his wallet. 'Put it back, Emerson,' Petersen said. 'They're on the house, *quid pro quo*.'

As he left the room Kenway walked straight into Margaret. 'You!' she said. 'In there again? Been having just one more shot, I suppose?'

'Wrong, Margaret. Come and sit down.' He pushed up a sleeve. 'Look, no marks. We've been talking business in there. I'm going to Manchester at midnight and have been engaged at no salary as a messenger for International

Entertainments Limited. Let's have a bottle of fizz.'

★ ★ ★

Kenway reached Euston at five minutes past midnight and bought a ticket to Manchester — a precaution in case the Inferno messenger accompanied him to the train-side to see him safely off, in which case he would have, perforce, to travel as far as the first stop from London.

He was in no doubt as to what were the contents of the brief-case so cleverly planted upon him. Talk of band parts and scripts which must be in Manchester tomorrow or the show could not go on would make nonsense to anyone with no more than elemental knowledge of show business; the show must have been rehearsed days ago — if there *was* a show at all — and that could not have been done without script or band parts. He felt in high spirits and self-congratulatory mood over the way in which he had played the part of Emerson, so that he

244

had become accepted by the club people.

With a little luck the brief-case he was to receive would be in the hands of Scotland Yard, and would no doubt be found to contain a supply of drugs, probably heroin for the Manchester area. He entered the restaurant, took a seat at the table on the left of the entrance and ordered coffee.

At 12.15 precisely a man appeared in the doorway, and stood looking round. He was tall and broadly built with a heavy moustache. A silk scarf was thrown round his neck. In his right hand was the brief-case. After a glance round he stepped over to the table. 'Mr. Emerson?' he queried, and in reply to Kenway's nod, said: 'Have to hand you this. Would you sign the receipt, please?'

Kenway did so, and the man left. The brief-case Kenway placed on a chair by his side. It was now 12.25 and he poured out the remainder of his pot of coffee and sugared it. A man who had been sitting at a neighbouring table pulled out a packet of cigarettes, selected one, and began feeling round in his pockets. He rose, crossed to Kenway and said: 'Excuse me, sir, could you oblige with a light?'

'Certainly!' Kenway flicked open his cigarette lighter and the man bent over the table to reach the flame with the end of his cigarette. 'Thanks,' he said. Kenway glanced at the clock, and rose to leave. He picked up the brief-case.

★ ★ ★

He opened his eyes to find a doctor and a waitress bending over him, and heard a voice coming, it seemed, from a distance, 'You all right, sir?' Coming to consciousness, he found he was lying on the floor with a woman supporting his head.

'What's happened?' he asked. 'Where the devil am I?'

'In the station restaurant, sir. You conked out. A customer saw you collapsing and tried to catch you before you fell,' the manager explained. 'He called us, and then had to hurry off to catch a train.'

'A train!' Kenway struggled up. 'I'm

better now,' he insisted and started peering round. 'Looking for something, sir?' the manager asked.

'My brief-case, where is it?'

'Brief-case? Haven't seen one, sir,'

He helped Kenway to the telephone. Kenway dialled. 'Petersen,' he said to the answering voice. 'Come over to the station restaurant quickly. It's Emerson.'

'The station restaurant! What the hell! Thought you were on that train.'

'Come down and you'll see why I'm not.'

Petersen listened to the manager's and waitress's account of what happened. He put Emerson into a taxi and then carried the story to Hookey, waiting in the Inferno.

'Jees!' Hookey said, blasphemously. 'Ten thousand quid's worth. The boss will be flaming. You don't think it was a set-up by Emerson?'

'You wouldn't think so had you seen him. He was out. Besides, he couldn't have arranged it in the time.'

'Well then Pete, there's been a leak somewhere. We'd better find it and stop it. A tall man in black he said? Know anybody like that?'

'Could be Lofty, one of the Liverpool lot. He's tall.'

'Right. Pass the word to the squad.'

28

Doctor Manson heard the story later in the morning in company with Superintendent Jones. Kenway presented the appearance of a man with a large hangover — and it wasn't only a physical hangover; he had, he knew, made a mess of a heaven-sent opportunity.

'Cor chase the crows to Jerusalem,' Jones ejaculated when the recital ended. 'Stone me. Just like a ruddy sucker, Kenny.' Kenway bridled. 'What do you mean — a ruddy sucker?'

'I kin see it as plain as if I'd bin there. He comes over to you an' asks for a light. He stood on your *left* side and when you flicks on the lighter, bends over you holding the cigarette to his mouth with his left hand, so as to reach the flame and hidin' the table from your sight. Right?'

'So far — yes. Go on.'

'O.K. So while he's holding the cigarette to the light with his left hand he drops a Mickey Finn in your flaming coffee with his *right* hand which you can't see. You're out in a minute. He calls for help, sees you bein' attended to, says he's in a hurry and walks off with the brief-case. Oldest trick in the world, Kenny, and you fell for it, hook, line and sinker. But if you hadn't had any coffee or booze he'd have chopped you on the back of the neck with a karate cut, called out that he'd seen you faint — and the result would have been just the same.'

'You think you were carrying heroin?' Manson asked.

'O' course he was carrying heroin or morphine.' Jones answered for him. 'You don't suppose he was hijacked for sheets of music. There's obviously a coupla drug mobs and one of 'em got a whisper.'

The Doctor who had been lost in thought for a space, came back to the present. 'You'd better not go to the club again, Kenway,' he said.

'Why not? Petersen accepted the story, vouched for by the restaurant people.'

'Because you'll be asked to carry another supply, somewhere.'

'I'd say a pretty strong 'no'.'

'Oh Lor!' Jones planted his hands on his knees and laughed uproariously. 'An' be told if you didn't they'd pass the word to the cops, *sub rosa*, that you were peddling drugs and then plant some on you. They don't know *you're* a cop. Remember to them you're Reginald Emerson an' have been buying heroin caps. That's gang methods, Kenny, whether its robbery with violence or anythin' else. Once you've taken part, however innocently, you're trapped. Blackmail is the biggest weapon in crime. Half the little crooks in the nick have been copped because they wus 'blacked' into doin' somethin' which the big noises knew was dangerous, and when the danger loomed the Noises walked out from the little ones. So don't you go into the club again.'

An hour later the A.C. put the question that had been exercising the mind of Doctor Manson: 'Pulling Petersen and the band leader in, Harry?'

'On what evidence, Edward? We've none beyond Kenway's. They'd deny everything — everything that is except the attack on him. To convict in any case we'd have to blow Kenway's identity, and that would alarm the entire organisation. Besides, the Inferno people have to get the stuff. They peddle it; we want the suppliers.'

Sir Edward scratched his head. 'God bless my soul,' he said. 'A nice confounded maze Barstowe's murder has led us into. He's a damned sight more nuisance dead than he was alive — and that's something, as you know.'

'He'll lead us into more trouble yet.'

'More? How?'

'You don't suppose they'll leave the loss of Kenway's brief-case without some action, do you? If the thing was only half full of heroin you can put the value of the contents at thousands of pounds. The Inferno crowd will have a pretty good idea of the identity of the hi-jackers, if not of the actual thief, and they'll be on the warpath. You'd better warn the uniformed branch to be on the look-out for trouble.'

Doctor Manson left, but it was half an hour before he returned to his study where Jones and Kenway were twiddling their thumbs, so to speak, and Sergeant Barratt was filing and indexing reports.

'Kenway, what time does the Inferno close?' he asked.

'Various times according to the customers remaining but at the latest, two-thirty.'

'What happens then?'

'Usually Petersen and Hookey go to the bank round the corner and dump the night's takings in the night safe.'

'And then? Is there a night watchman?'

'Don't know, Doctor. I've never been there after they've closed.'

The Doctor looked at Jones, who nodded. 'Want me to case the joint?'

'Yes. Any watchman, any burglar alarms, type of locks on doors. Is there a back entrance? You, Kenway, draw me a plan of the manager's office since you've been in there a number of times. I want to study the fittings and the furniture.'

'Goin' to break into the joint?' Jones asked.

'On permission from the Home Secretary.'

'The Home Sec. What the — ?' Doctor

Manson had made no answer, but walked out. It took the fat superintendent the remainder of the day to gain the reliable information asked for, and with Mackinnon he paid a visit to the club during the evening. 'Just a routine visit, Mr. Petersen,' Mackinnon announced, and accompanied him into the office. 'Inspection at intervals, as you know is required by law.'

'Fire exits all right!' Jones reported, tongue in cheek. 'Burglar alarms?'

'Direct communication with the West End station, Superintendent,' Petersen assured him.

'Excellent idea . . . quick response . . . Where?'

The manager showed him. 'Switch inside the front door. Switched on when we leave for the night.'

During the afternoon of the following day Kenway visited Margaret at the Maida Vale flat. 'You win,' he told her. 'I'm not going to the club any more.' She pirouetted. 'I'm glad,' she said, 'but why the change of mind?' He told her of the restaurant episode. 'You didn't know about it?' he queried.

'No, not a word has been mentioned in the club. Oh, my God, they must have lost thousands. What made you so foolish as to take the case?'

'Well, it seemed all right as they put it. I happened to be in the office — '

'You believe that?'

'Believe it — why shouldn't I?'

'Because, my dear boy, it was obviously planned. Had you not been in the office they would have invited you on some excuse. It didn't matter which night the stuff went. They wanted Manchester and they knew you went backwards and forwards there, and were not likely to be suspected. They've never lost anything before, so far as I know.' She hesitated and wrinkled her brows. 'Unless . . . Aaronson,' she said.

'Aaronson? What about him? Do you mean — '

'I know he made two journeys.'

'And he hasn't been seen since.'

'Perhaps, like you, he breezed off.'

'Or perhaps he didn't — or couldn't. I must go now, Margaret. I'll not be in the club again but I'll keep in touch with you here, and we'll have another day out.'

A Manson very disturbed in mind listened to Kenway's version of the talk with the girl. 'Death is a great silencer,' he said, 'but what can they have done with the body?'

★　★　★

Seven men sat ill at ease in the room of Chief Detective Inspector Mackinnon in Scotland Yard. It was turned 2.30 in the morning and they were hopefully awaiting a telephone call. It trilled at a few moments to three o'clock. 'All Sir Garnet,' a voice said.

Doctor Manson stood up. 'Move in,' he ordered. Bowles was the first to leave. Bowles was the Yard's expert in locks and bolts. There was not in existence any lock, key or combination that could withstand his ingenuity given time. As a burglar he could have lifted thousands of pounds in money, jewellery and what have you. He knew the secret of every manner of lock. He also knew Scotland Yard men — which is why he never attempted to lift thousands of pounds in money, jewellery and what have you.

'Give me a quarter of an hour, Doctor,' he said as he left the Yard.

He cut through the Embankment Gardens, across the Strand and into Regent Street, slipped into the doorway of a block, went through an office by arrangement with the tenant, down the basement — and found himself in a small backyard with a narrow passage leading out to a street parallel with Regent Street. The yard served as a private backway entrance and had two doors, the one from which Bowles emerged, and the other the back door of the Inferno Club. A few moments' fiddling with the latter's lock and he entered the club.

The burglar alarm had been disconnected in the West End station on orders, so no warning of the entry had been sounded. Bowles as an extra precaution turned off the alarm switch and then opened the front door of the club. One by one at intervals the remaining six waiting men descended the stairs to the entrance of the club. With gloved hands they searched meticulously, carefully replacing each article exactly as it was found before being moved. The club, being a basement, had no windows, and the searchers were able to work with lights.

The search was negative so far as finding evidence of the presence or the distribution of drugs were concerned. It was not, however, without success in another direction. When the Yard's officers left around four o'clock the manager's office had been very completely 'bugged' for listening to conversations — with a listening post established, with the co-operation of a firm on the ground-floor and immediately above the club. Two constable shorthand writers in plain clothes were to take turns sitting in a small store room of the firm, and were to have the assistance of a tape recorder for a permanent and authoritative record of everything said.

29

The Permanent Under Secretary at the Foreign Office tapped on his desk, beating a thin tattoo with a gold revolving pencil. He was a tall, slim figure, elegant in black jacket and waistcoat with white collar and a grey cravat, and grey striped trousers — the traditional garb of Establishment. He was thinking — having no common or ordinary Civil Servant to do the thinking for him at the moment. On the opposite side of the desk sat Mr. Wilfred Saunderson, an executive member of the Commission on Narcotic Drugs of the United Nations Organisation, working in conjunction with the Narcotic Bureau of New York.

He had just concluded the narration of a curious story and was requesting the assistance of the Foreign Office in elucidating a problem causing the Bureau great concern.

The pencil tapping ceased at last and

the P.U.S. squared his decision — which was not forthwith to decline assistance to U.N.O. but, as is the habit of government departments, to pass the buck as it were to some other branch of the Establishment — an operation, it may be stated, at which Permanent Under Secretaries are adroit beyond belief.

'It is true, sir, that we have had a number of resignations from this Department,' he said, with an obvious capital 'D', 'but I am afraid that we cannot associate any one of them with your story, except one, who is dead.'

'But — ' the visitor began. The P.U.S. waved an elegantly manicured hand. 'I suggest you try the Secretary of State for the Home Office, or the Commissioner of Police for the Metropolitan Area. I think, perhaps, the latter would be the more satisfactory for you.' The Permanent Under Secretary pushed a desk button and the visitor was ushered out.

Having been thus shunted from Downing Street to Victoria Street he was, half an hour later, in a further shunting operation from the Commissioner of

Police up a further flight of stairs to the Assistant Commissioner (Crime). Sir Edward Allen, having heard no more than three or four sentences of the tale, sent hurriedly for Doctor Manson. 'Listen to this, Commander,' he enjoined, after introductions had been made.

'Some two years ago,' Mr. Saunderson began, 'the United Nations Commission on Narcotic Drugs was approached by an Englishman with an offer to investigate and provide information of a widespread organisation for supplying drugs of addiction, the existence of which he had learned by chance. He gave us certain detail which we knew to be true because we already had it in our possession. But there was a lot more about which we were unaware.

'He was a man who quite obviously knew what he was talking about and he had extensive contacts in foreign countries, travelling abroad a great deal. He was, he said, convinced that drugs were being obtained in Britain and were being sent across the Atlantic. He wanted to trace the source of that supply.

'We suggested that he got in touch with the British narcotics people, but he said he would rather not do that since any known connection by him with people dealing with narcotics would quickly become known to the people concerned in the illegal traffic, and would mitigate against the success of his efforts.

'Well, to cut a long story short we attached him to the staff of the U.N.O. Commission. He did not want a salary, which was a pleasant surprise from our point of view. All he needed was expenses. In the course of the next few months he sent us detailed reports of operations, names and places that led to the arrest of a complete drug organisation in France. Each month we received from him reports which he asked should not be made public: circumstantial evidence of organisation methods, of dealers, exporters and importers which we acted upon. We, in turn, furnished him with certain matters, sending them to an address and in a name which he told us was not his own — but I'll come to that later.

'Four months ago he wrote to us rather excitedly that he was on the track of something of the utmost importance. A fortnight later he said the 'something' was a plan to flood America with drugs. Arrangements were in the making by the 'Boss' of a drug trafficking organisation in America. They had, he said, already imported quite a lot under cover of licences to import. He added that he knew one of the heads of the organisation in Britain that had the supplies and the distribution and was connected with a club. He was, he said, working under very close cover and when he sent us names and addresses would we suggest that such information had come through Interpol, since if it was thought that a British source was the culprit he did not think that his identity could be concealed and he would be in danger.'

Mr. Saunderson put his elbows on the desk and leaned over them. He spoke slowly and very distinctly. 'From that moment we have heard nothing,' he said — and sombrely. 'We have written asking urgently for some communication of any kind. You have heard, of course, of the large amount of heroin seized on New York dockside. It seemed to bear out the information sent to us.

'The Commission, worried over the extent suggested by our representative, sent me over to see whether anything had gone amiss. I went to the address to which we had sent letters; it was a top room in an office building in Acton. The room was locked. In response to my fears that the occupant might be ill or dead, the commissionaire opened the door with a master key. Gentlemen, our letters were strewn on the floor inside, the envelopes unopened.'

The A.C. and Doctor Manson digested slowly the statement, looking across at each other. 'And you want . . . ?' the A.C. began.

'To help find the man and get his story.'

'Um. It is, Mr. Saunderson, hardly a police affair at this stage, you know. He may have become scared at something — been suspected — and knowing he was in danger just fled and could be lying low.

He has committed no offence and we can hardly make a police search without some material evidence.'

'You have not told us his name, Mr. Saunderson,' Manson pointed out.

'We do not know his real name, Mr. Commander. He would not disclose it lest in some way it might leak out — he regarded anonymity as a necessary precaution. The name he, and we, used was Arnold Aaronson.'

It shook the police executives. 'Aaronson!' shouted the A.C.

Mr. Saunderson shot up in his chair. 'You *know* him?'

The A.C. waved a hand in the air. It looked like an invocation to the Deity.

'Oh, Lord,' he said. 'Tell him, Harry.'

Manson said: 'Was there any disturbance or signs of violence at that Acton address?'

'None at all. A typewriter was on the table. Everything seemed to be in order, including a file containing copies of letters which he had written to us. But you say you know him.'

'Know *of* him, Mr. Saunderson. It is a

peculiar story and begins with a man who seemed to have unaccountably committed suicide in a London club, but who, it was found, had been murdered. I am head of Scotland Yard's Homicide Squad, and on investigation of the dead man's belongings we came across a receipt made out to 'Mr. Aaronson'. The address on the receipt was a slum. At it we found materials for injecting heroin, and a quantity of the drug itself. We also found a membership card for a club called the Inferno.

'There was nobody in the room, but we subsequently found that there *had* been a body, and that two men, both criminals, had been paid to remove and dump it into a barge in the Thames. One of the men was later found stabbed to death and the other came to us for protection. It was he who told us of the removal of a body. Aaronson had been the tenant of the room, but the dead man we subsequently discovered was not Aaronson. We do not know who he is, or was. The obvious conclusion is, of course, that Aaronson killed the man and has fled, but it might well be that a third person is involved; that he disposed of the man and then he and Aaronson fled. We have been searching for Aaronson unsuccessfully.'

Mr. Saunderson scratched his head in some perplexity. His face bore an anxious expression. 'Look,' he said, 'he was on the verge of a discovery of vast importance. We want his information. Have you circulated Aaronson's description and photograph to the Press?'

The A.C. frowned. 'We are not without that knowledge, Mr. Saunderson,' he protested. 'But the fact is Aaronson was a complete mystery. We do not possess a description or a photograph of him. All we know is that he was a big man — whatever that may mean.'

'Hah!' The exclamation came like a shot from Saunderson. 'I can help you there. I have a photograph of Aaronson taken for our identification files; and also a physical description.' He opened his case, peered into the interior, fiddled around, and finally picked out a photograph which he placed on the desk. 'This is Aaronson,' he said.

Sir Edward picked it up to examine it. It dropped from his fingers and fell face downwards on the desk. His monocle fell from his good left eye. He looked dazed, with his mouth opening and shutting. Manson rose in alarm. 'What is wrong, Edward?' he said. 'What's the matter with you?'

Sir Edward lay slouched back in the chair and pointed to the photograph. The Doctor lifted and turned it over — and recoiled as though he had been shot.

The portrait was of Frederick Barstowe.

'My God! My God!' Manson said.

30

For five days a relay of typists at the listening post attached to the bugged management office of the Inferno Club heard and recorded nothing of particular interest. There were conversations from which it was pretty obvious that drugs were passed, and the typed recordings might be valuable at some future time. On the sixth day, however, a very odd conversation was overheard. It was cryptic, except to watchful and very suspicious police officers.

The shorthand transcriptions of three telephone calls, together with the recordings were taken to Doctor Manson and Chief Inspector Mackinnon; and from there went to the A.C. in conference. Sir Edward was not a little dubious. 'Pretty nebulous, Doctor, isn't it?' he queried. 'It's a lead, A.C. and linking two centres,' Manson retorted — and got the authority he sought.

The Doctor took the news to Inspector Wellbeing of the Narcotics Squad and made certain suggestions which found support from the inspector. 'Do we make arrangements with the port authorities?' he asked.

'Good heavens, no. It would be all over the dockside in a few minutes. We go to work quietly.'

At Lloyd's, Wellbeing was told that a cargo vessel *Eastern Star* was due in from Singapore in two days' time, but would arrive well after dark. The vessel did, in fact, arrive on time. Dockers had ceased work and unloading was, accordingly, not to start until the following morning.

At midnight detectives who had entered the dockyard secretly were perched sixty feet up at the top of dockland cranes, and behind chimney stacks on the roofs of sheds. They were equipped with powerful night glasses and 2-way radios. Outside the dock gates, and discreetly hidden, more detectives waited in squad cars.

For an hour the watchers peered through the eerie moonlight and the mist at the *Eastern Star* rising and falling with the movement of the water. She was in darkness except for her riding lights. At one-thirty a radio crackled in Scotland Yard. From the top of one of the cranes a detective in the shelter of a driving cabin said, softly: 'A man is leaving the boat.' A moment later he said: 'He is moving towards a stationary shooting brake.' Another pause and then: 'Just driving off.' From the Yard Mackinnon radioed the squad cars outside both gates of the yard: 'Let the brake get clear of the gates and then stop it. But don't lose it. We're on our way.'

The police swooped. The station brake driven by a Chinaman named Kwang Lee was escorted to the Yard and there searched. In a specially constructed compartment under the brake floor-boards opium was found. Put on scales it weighed forty pounds. Inspector Wellbeing whistled.

'What is it worth?' Manson asked.

'As opium for pipe-smoking or for reefer cigarettes, several thousands of pounds.' He hesitated and added: 'For conversion into the hard drugs of addiction, particularly heroin, and in the black market, between £30,000 and £40,000.'

'S'truth,' ejaculated Old Fat Man who, sitting in a chair had hard work to keep his eyes open during the long waiting hours of the night. 'It's the wrong flaming job we're in, Doctor.' He picked up a shred of the opium. 'I'll take six pennorth. Hey, you,' he roared at the Chinese driver. 'Where was you a'takin' this van?' Kwang Lee shrank back at the size of him and at the ferocious gaze a few inches from his face. In a mixture of pidgin English and Chinese interpreted by Inspector Wellbeing who had a speaking knowledge of Cantonese, Kwang Lee said he knew the spot but not the name of the place. On a map he pointed out a junction of the North Circular Road with Watling Street. Pressed as to how he knew the road, he said he had made several trips there over the past few months. To further questions he said that at the junction he was met by a car and driver and the opium was transferred. He did not know where the other car journeyed to. Nor did he know to whom belonged the shooting brake he had driven each time. He picked it up on the dockside where it was left parked.

The registration plates were useless as a means of identification; investigation showed that the letters and numbers had been issued to a private owner in Fowey, Cornwall, who was still using them on his Bentley which had not left the area for months.

Doctor Manson himself, with Inspector Mackinnon, went to the listening post at 9.30. He thought that a bugged conversation might be of considerable interest in the circumstances since news of the non-arrival of the brake van where it was expected would have become known. It was! The first call came a few moments after ten o'clock at which hour the manager came on duty.

'Petersen (came a voice over the telephone) 'what the hell happened last night?'

'Last night, sir? Nothing.'

'Then why has not the cargo been despatched?'

'N . . . not d . . . d . . . espatched. I don't understand. The conveyance was left. Do you mean — ?'

'I mean we haven't seen it. The car went to the rendezvous.'

'I don't — '

'Who was driving?'

'Lee, as usual. I'll inquire.'

'Inquire nothing. And don't use the telephone at your end. We'll make inquiries.'

The call could not be traced. 'It came from a call box with dialling system, sir,' the Exchange explained.

'Damn all call boxes,' the Doctor said. A few calls which followed were concerned with club business matters, and it was not until an hour had passed that the voice came on again.

'Lee is not on the ship. He hasn't been seen since yesterday and there is no sign of the brake.'

'Oh, God. Do you think he's skipped with the stuff? I'll see what I can find out.'

'See nothing. Keep quiet and leave it to us.'

'That has put them into a flap — whoever they are,' the Doctor said, chuckling. He went to the A.C. with an idea. Sir Edward looked dubious. 'It's the *advocatus diaboli*, Harry.'

'So? I'll quote Paul to you, Edward: 'Let us do evil that good may come'.' The A.C. agreed, doubtfully. So Jones visited Kwang Lee in the cells and spoke very distinctly. 'You ... know ... prison ... clink ... nick, soon?' he asked, and Lee nodded. 'You'll ... be ... in prison ... nick ... for seven years.' He counted seven on his fingers; and Lee nearly collapsed. At this Old Fat Man explained painfully how it might be possible to get Lee out of his trouble if he could tell how much, and how often, and where opium was smuggled into Britain — and Jones could get blood out of a stone!

He carried the news back to the

Doctor. 'Lumme,' he reported, 'it's comin' in all over the flamin' place — here, in Southampton, Liverpool and Glasgow.'

'Same way, Fat Man?'

'Sure. There's Kwang Lee (him we've got) Li Lang, and Fa Chein, all boatswains, on ships coming from the East. They get fifty quid a passage for handling the doings. But that's all they know — the spot to run the stuff to — the same spot each time they dock.'

31

So Aaronson was now known to be, or to have been Frederick Barstowe. And Barstowe had been killed in an exclusive club in the heart of the West End. There was still no clue to his attacker, or to how the attacker could have entered the club unseen, committed the shooting, left the revolver by the side of the dead man after rolling his fingerprints on it, locking the room door and walking out of the club again unseen, unsuspected.

The puzzle of the rent receipt made out to Aaronson and found in Barstowe's possession was solved with the knowledge that he had been Aaronson. Why the fastidious Barstowe was housing himself in the dockside hovel at various times, was also explained by his communication to the Narcotics Commission that he was working under close cover. It was obvious, Manson thought, that the 'important discovery' was the smuggling of drugs into the port in the way that they had now discovered for themselves. But it did not explain the death of the man who had been killed in the Water Street room. Medical and post mortem examination showed that he had died before Barstowe.

The A.C. put up an explanation: 'Barstowe found him there, realised that his disguise had been rumbled and killed him. Then the man's friends outed Barstowe in revenge.'

Manson shook his head. 'You saw the body of the man found in the barge. Do you think he was the type of man who could have gained entry into the Dilettantes' Club?'

'Then how, and why?'

'I think the man was killed in mistake — a mistake that was afterwards rectified.'

'In mistake for Barstowe?'

'By someone who had in some way penetrated his identity, realised the reason for the disguise, and went there expecting that the man he saw inside was Barstowe in disguise.'

'By whom?'

'By the man who later in the pub offered two men £50 to take the body away, and who, going down into the barge to see that the body was safely stowed away suddenly realised that it was not that of Barstowe. Knowing that the Aaronson disguise *was* Barstowe he finished the job later.'

'Why?'

'Because he, the murderer, was engaged in the smuggling, was likely a key figure and realised that Barstowe had made that 'important discovery'.'

The A.C. pondered the problem. 'I see . . . and then stabbed the man at Brighton and went after the second man, because . . . '

'Because both had seen him, knew that the body they had moved was that of a *murdered* man, and could identify him — yes, Edward.'

★   ★   ★

Doctor Manson took Jones with him and drove to the junction of the North Circular Road and Watling Street where

Kwang Lee said his cargo was always transferred to another vehicle. Continued close questioning had failed to extract any further useful information. His instructions, he said, were to drive to the rendezvous, sit in the car and keep his eyes from wandering. The rendezvous car drove up behind him and the cargo was transferred.

'Which way did the car drive off afterwards?' he was asked.

'I don't know,' Lee said; and explained in his pidgin English, 'I always had to drive away first.' It was good planning, the Doctor thought. Nobody knew anything except his own little part in the complete operation. It was likely, he thought, that the goods might be transferred two or three times, leaving the end of the trail quite cold.

At the junction the Doctor took stock of his surroundings. They were pleasant enough but gave him little comfort. The crossing gave access to routes which could run to all parts of the compass — north, south, east and west. About 300 yards away lay Hendon Stadium,

Cricklewood, Wembley, Hampstead and Golders Green were on routes in various directions, any one of which could have been taken by the rendezvous car and from which the whole South of England could have been easily reached. The description of the car given by Lee was that it was black with a sloping bonnet and a small radiator; it sounded, Jones said, like a Jaguar.

The Doctor crossed with Jones the Brent River bridge and let his eyes wander. In front of him stretched a placid waste of water some two miles long and half a mile at its widest part. The Metropolitan Water Board calls it the Brent Reservoir, but nobody else does; its universal name is the Welsh Harp. The title has been appropriated — nobody knows now by whom — because it was, and always had been, the name of an old public house standing in a fork of the Brent River; the Welsh Harp hostelry was always a popular resort of Londoners. Now, the Welsh Harp description has been applied to the water, and stands adrift from the hostelry. It is the watering place of North West London, a pleasant vista of water with on the opposite side verdant open spaces, the picnic grounds of Londoners, and a miniature golf course.

With their backs to the public house, the two detectives watched the amateurish yachtsmen tacking in dinghies a hazardous way over the water, crew novices, flailing oars in rowboats, pleasant parties of people reclining on the greensward — a little sylvan paradise is the Welsh Harp on such days.

★　★　★

When the laboratory men examined the yellow brake van after it had been brought from the docks to Scotland Yard with the Chinaman, Kwang Lee a prisoner, they found traces of mud on the floorboards and a few leaves of *algae*. Put under a microscope by Chief Inspector Merry, the Deputy Scientist, the mud proved to be river mud with traces of chalk; and the *algae* when compared with samples in the laboratory library of specimens was obviously *Elodea Canadensis*, called by the unscholarly water thyme.

'Found in rivers,' Doctor Manson said, and told it to Jones. 'That's funny,' Jones said. Manson alerted and looked at him. 'How come?' he asked. Jones, who knew his London explained. 'There's a river and water at the junction. Now, that Chink says he drove the brake to the junction of the roads and sat there waiting, keeping his eyes from wandering, until a car transferred the stuff. Then he had to drive off. *Then how comes it that there were river mud and weeds on his floorboards, since he never got out?*'

'You mean that they were on the floorboards already?' the Doctor said.

'That's how I see it.'

It was this conclusion that had taken Jones and the Doctor to the junction of the roads — to find what he had not expected — the reservoir and a river, and it was because of this that he was searching mentally and physically the Welsh Harp and the River Brent which fed water to the reservoir.

Opening his case — the Box of Tricks as it had been named years before — he took from it various articles and a trowel; and with these, collected samples of mud from the banks of the river and the shores of the reservoir, and a little of the floating weed. Each sample was placed in a plastic container. An hour later, examination through his comparison microscope made it plain that his collection matched in every detail the mud and *algae* taken from the banks.

Meanwhile, Mackinnon had been involved in other operations.

There is little glamour in detection. It has been held by a great C.I.D. officer that success in detective work is from ten per cent inspiration, ten per cent luck, and eighty per cent plodding hard work. Mackinnon was engaged in the hard work. He concentrated on the car which met the brake van on those nights when the opium was run, and which Jones had considered to be a black Jaguar. The description by Kwang Lee was the only clue the Yard had.

For hours, clerks in the Motor Taxation office waded through the list of owners who had licensed black Jaguars, recording their names and addresses. They ran into three figures in the Metropolitan area. Mackinnon and his staff divided them into the various boroughs. Detectives from the local C.I.D.s visited and checked the owners, the car users, and the direction in which they were usually driven. Garages were quizzed over any repairs done to Jaguars, and on a sudden inspiration from Kenway, any repairs carried out on a yellow coloured brake van the number (faked) of which was supplied.

Which is where Lady Luck turned up with her ten per cent contribution; a foreman in a garage on the outskirts of Hendon reported that he had worked on a car answering the brake's description. Driven to Scotland Yard he eyed the van, lifted the bonnet, and examined an inside part. 'That's the job,' he said, and pointed out the reason for identification. There, however, the luck ended.

'Who is the owner?' Mackinnon asked.

'Search me,' was the reply. 'He just drove in, said the engine was misfiring, and I put it right.'

'Don't you take names?'

'Nah, guv'nor, not when someone comes in with a little job, waits, and then pays cash.'

'Hendon,' Manson said when he heard. 'That's only a quarter of a mile from the junction.' The mud and the weeds seemed to be falling into place. 'If it runs round there — '

'I'll have a hunt,' said Kenway.

'No. *I'll* take a look-see. Don't wanna raise an alarm, Kenny.'

Jones went — and called at a school playground during the morning play break. He shouted 'Hi!' and the sight of the big fat man with a baby-like face brought attention. 'Any of you lot take down the numbers of cars?'

'Yes sir.' The reply came from two lads aged round about twelve.

'Got your books, son?' They produced them from jacket pockets.

'Ah, let's go through 'em.'

'What for?' Jones drew them on one side, stared round conspiratorially, then whispered: 'It's a secret, son, but we must find a certain car.'

'Coo!' said the boys.

'Not a word about it, mind.' They went through the pages of the books, and Jones picked out the number of the brake.

'That . . . ? That's a yellow Morris, a van,' one of the boys said.

'Ha, how do you know it's a Morris?' (it was, as a matter of fact).

'Cor, anyone can recognise a Morris.'

'Reckon you don't know where you took the number?' Jones said challengingly.

'Reckon I do, Mister. I see it at the gates of Wilson's factory past the swimming pool when I was coming home from Scouts.'

'What time would that be?'

'Ten o'clock on a Wednesday night, Mister. Scouts is always on a Wednesday.'

Doctor Manson heard the account with a chuckle at the ingenuity of Jones. 'I don't know anybody but you, Fat Man, with the mind of a child. What made you think of collectors of numbers?'

'H'observation . . . I'm allus observin'
things and puttin' 'em in me mind.'

'Well, whaddyer know! He's got something in his mind,' Kenway said.

32

'Out of the mouths of babes and sucklings,' Doctor Manson said.

'Eh?' The A.C. appeared a little bewildered.

'And a little child shall lead them.'

Sir Edward screwed a monocle into his left eye and surveyed his visitor through it. 'Are you all right, Harry?' he requested.

'Better than I've been for some time, Edward.' Scrutinising him closely the A.C. was inclined to agree. Wrinkles had been erased from the broad, high forehead, and the creases which stretched out from the corners of his eyes when he was worried over a case had smoothed out. The eyes themselves were bright, instead of being sunk in their deep sockets. The A.C. himself felt lighter at the signs. 'Something happened?' he asked.

'Something has *occurred*' came the

reply 'and quite a time before our killings. A twelve-year-old schoolboy returning home late at night saw a motor vehicle with a registration number he hadn't picked up before for his collection. It was the number of a yellow brake — the false registration and extinct number. The brake was emerging from the gate of Wilson's factory, a quarter of a mile from the Welsh Harp and from the mud and *algae* we found in it.'

He told Jones's story. 'We've been trying to trace that van with all the police force working, without success — and a little child leads us to it. The van is worth at least £700. We have it, and not a soul has inquired about it. Why not?'

'False number plates.'

'Put on for the night journeys to the docks when required. Number plates are removable, you know. Now Wilson's factory has five motor vehicles registered — two cars, two closed lorries and a yellow brake van, ANO259. Now for what reason is a yellow van with a faked registration coming out of a closed factory at ten o'clock at night?'

'What is produced at the factory?' the A.C. asked.

'Plastics. And that means they use nitric and sulphuric acids, nitro-cellulose, camphor, alcohol and nitrogen, denity-benzine, caustic alkali and ammonia — and there's a hell of a stink to it all.'

'You think heroin is in the place?'

'I think more than that. Let me say that I think I can reconcile the conflicting views of Inspector Wellbeing and Superintendent Johns. Each of them is right — in his own way.'

'And you want — ?'

'I want to know all about the Wilson factory. We'd better get Baxter on to it.'

The Yard's City expert reported that Wilsons had been established just over four years with three directors, one of whom was the managing director and general manager.

'Can we get inside the place?' Manson asked; and received the reply: 'Nothing easier.'

The factory was situated at that extension of the Welsh Harp which runs under Cold Oak Lane and which proceeds in a narrow neck alongside York Park, past streets which go off at right angles, ending with Argyle Road and Ramsay Road. Beyond this is open space alongside a canal.

A Factories Inspector and his assistant went thoroughly over the factory, finding a little fault here and there, but generally expressing satisfaction at the protective treatment arrangements for the workers' safety, which were received with gratification by the managing director. They wandered among the various processes.

The Ministry of Labour, both national and local, would have been at a loss to recognise their inspectors, either by sight or name; had the inspectors been challenged they would have been hard put to it to establish their professional identity. They were, however, doing a thorough job of work.

'You, of course, carry out experiments with a view to improving the products?' the elder of the two suggested.

'Of course.'

'With adequate precautions in regard to the various chemicals, etc. used in the manufacture of plastics?'

'Oh, indeed. We have a laboratory in which we test the quality of our goods, and search for new methods of manufacture.'

'The laboratory is — where? Not in the factory itself, I hope.'

The manager led the way to a brick building separated from the actual factory, but with a covered connecting passage. 'Only the two senior directors are allowed in here to ensure that none of the various poisonous substances get into wrong hands — by mistake, of course.'

'Of course. We had better, I think, see that the usual precautions are in force.'

The manager, though in some doubt, unlocked the door. The laboratory was housed in a single storey — a large square room well equipped with, leading off it, another smaller room. Glass-fronted shelves held jars, test tubes and beakers. An electric furnace occupied a space in one corner and extensive chemical machinery occupied benches. The second room had wicker-covered carboys of sulphuric acid, nitric acid and commercial alcohol; and a variety of other chemicals and reagents were on wide, tin-lined shelves. Overall hovered a reek bitter to the olfactory senses. 'It's a smelly business, plastics, you know,' the manager intimated.

'Quite,' the chief factory inspector said. He looked across at his assistant, who led the manager back into the outer room and engaged him in inquiry. Left alone, the chief peered among the chemicals, reading off the names on the various porcelain holders, inspected the various sets of apparatus, and finally took samples of dust from the test benches. From white overalls hanging on a peg he quickly emptied the pockets on to a bench and gathered the dust and fluff into a cellulose envelope taken from the small case he carried. Then he rejoined his colleague and the manager in the outer room. 'Well, all seems satisfactory,' he announced. 'Oh, you'll have a garage, of course.'

'Back of the drive.' The manager led the way. 'Let me see,' the inspector said. 'Er . . . two cars, two lorries and a yellow van. That right?'

'No van. We sold that, having no need for it.'

The chief inspector gave a final scrutiny of papers which he was carrying 'Three directors, I see — J.B. Wilson, S. W. Wilson and yourself, who is also general manager. I take it the other directors are not present?'

'No, sir. I am the operative director. The Wilsons are purely scientific. One is generally here in the evenings when things are quiet and they can concentrate on experiments in plastics.'

'Quite so. You will, I take it inform them of this inspection?'

In Scotland Yard the factory inspectors came out of their chrysalis as Doctor Manson and Chief Inspector Wellbeing of Narcotics. From his case the Doctor abstracted the cellophane envelopes in which were the samples of dust taken from the laboratory benches and from the pockets of the overall. The dust was sent for analysis to Chief Inspector Merry, the Deputy Scientist.

To the A.C. the doctor detailed the equipment of the factory laboratory. 'It contained,' he said, 'large quantities of nitric and sulphuric acid, nitro-cellulose, camphor — '

'Camphor?' Sir Edward queried.

'Camphor, yes. Essential to transform the cellulose pulp into stiff dough, like baker's dough, ready for moulding into plastic articles. There was also a considerable quantity of acetic anhydride . . . ' He paused.

'Do I sense some emphasis on the last-named, Harry?'

'You do.' Edward. Acetic anhydride is the reagent for the acetylisation of morphine to produce heroin. I know of no reason for its presence in quantity in a plastics concern, especially when it is in the company of dehydrating and other apparatus which can be used in the process of converting opium into morphine and thence, into heroin. Samples of dust which I brought along bear traces, under laboratory examination and analysis of both morphine and heroin. A smell which permeated the laboratory — into which only the Wilson directors enter — is that given off by raw opium.

'In short, Edward, the factory I am quite sure, is producing, unknown to its plastics side, heroin and morphine from raw opium, which is imported secretly as we have learned through the discovery of the van, through Kwang Lee, and through Liverpool, Southampton and Glasgow.'

'God bless my soul!' the A.C. ejaculated, and blew his nose violently. 'And the general manager?'

'Knows nothing about it or he wouldn't have shown us so much. He explained that the directors visited the factory only in the evenings when there was no machinery working and no noises to distract them from their experiments, as good a secret cover as I could imagine!'

'And the heroin?'

'Exported as we know to America and distributed in this country through the Inferno and allied clubs. I have no doubt at all that the Wilsons — if there are any — are A. Abrahams and Co., Ltd., the exporting agents.'

33

Petersen and Hookey (real name Sergius Salsburg) totted up the night's takings in the Inferno Club, put them securely away in the safe. They closed up the office, turned out the lights, switched on the burglar alarm, double-locked the front door, walked together up the stairs to the street — and into the arms of the waiting Superintendent Jones and Chief Inspector Mackinnon.

'Mr. Petersen and Mr. Salsburg?' Jones queried. 'I must ask you to accompany us to Scotland Yard for inquiries.'

'Concerning what?' Petersen wanted to know.

'They'll tell you at the Yard, gentlemen.' It was 2.30 a.m.

A fuming Petersen looked round the interview room at Central Office. Doctor Manson and Inspector Wellbeing sat behind a table desk and were joined by Mackinnon. Kenway had been in the charge room when the couple were brought in. Hookey, seeing him, stepped to his side, talked in a whisper out of the side of his mouth: 'You, too? Don't say anything, Emerson. We'll get you out of this, whatever it is.'

'What is the reason for this outrage?' Petersen, storming with rage rapped out the question at the table. 'And after a hard night's work. I am the manager of a well-known club. If you wanted me at any time you knew where to find me. Why are we brought in here at this hour?'

'To save creating a scene by arresting you at the club during hours,' Manson said.

'Arrest? On what charge?'

'Being at various times in possession of drugs in contravention of the Dangerous Drugs Act, 1951, and dealing unlawfully in such drugs, namely, heroin.'

'Nonsense! We have nothing to do with drugs. You have already raided the club once without finding anything on the premises.' He pointed at Kenway. 'You arrested Emerson, here.' Kenway stepped round the table and stood behind Manson.

'This, Petersen,' the Doctor said, 'is Detective Chief Inspector Kenway, of the C.I.D. You have sold him heroin on four occasions.'

The pair gazed at Kenway, thunderstruck, for some moments. Then Petersen, almost screaming with rage, shouted; 'You . . . you . . . you bloody police spy . . . you . . . '

'That will do,' Jones said. 'Listen.'

Doctor Manson put a tape recorder on the table. 'I want you, Petersen, to listen to tape recordings of certain telephone calls.' He switched on the machine.

Petersen . . . tonight, you know where. After midnight.

Right, sir.

Petersen . . . what the hell happened last night? . . .

Last night, sir. Nothing . . .

Then why has not the cargo been despatched . . .

Not despatched. I don't understand.

The conveyance was left. Do you mean? . . .

I mean we haven't seen it.

Doctor Manson switched off the machine. 'No. Petersen,' he said, 'Lee did not go off with the stuff. We picked up the Chinaman and the yellow van and the opium. We still have them.' He eyed the club manager. 'You and, you, too, Salsburg, are in deep waters. We know that opium has been smuggled in in large quantities through London and other places, and has been turned into heroin. We realise that you are underlings acting under orders — that you are small fry. Now who, Petersen, is the 'sir' of the telephone talks?'

'I don't know.'

'There *is* an organisation?'

Petersen shrugged his shoulders. 'If there was,' he said, 'it's busted now.'

Doctor Manson leaned forward on the table. 'Sit down, Petersen.' Kenway brought forward two chairs. 'Now two, probably three, men have been murdered by this organisation. One was Aaronson, who you knew very well. You can both be charged as accessories before or after the fact. I make no promises but you may do yourself a bit of good. We want the name of the head of this vicious organisation. Who is he?'

'Sir, I do not know.' Manson threw his hands in the air. 'Take them away,' he ordered.

Hookey said, 'Will you listen to me, sir? Petersen is quite correct. He doesn't know. And I really don't know. We receive telephone messages, always at night. They convey certain instructions. The voice we have been told is that of 'The Boss' — that is the word used. We have never seen him so far as we know. All we know is a voice.'

'What number do you call when you want to telephone?'

'We don't know. We haven't a number. In view of what you have said about murder, if I knew anything, I would tell you. That is the gospel truth sir. Selling drugs — that is a minor offence. But murder — no.'

They were taken to the cells.

'Do you believe them?' the A.C. asked later in the morning.

'Yes,' Manson replied, 'I do. The Boss, as they call him would not want anyone to be able to put a finger on him.'

'Then we are just where we were before!'

The Doctor smiled. 'I have, I think, an idea that may put mortal fright into him or them.'

The 'fright' appeared in the final edition of the London evening papers in black type under large headings. *The Record* had the best report:

DRUG RING SENSATION STARTLING REVELATIONS OF MASSIVE MANUFACTURE

Scotland Yard's Narcotic officers have uncovered an organisation engaged in producing heroin in large quantities from raw opium smuggled into Britain in cargo goods.

The first clue was the seizure of a yellow van driven by a Chinese, which was found to contain forty pounds of opium. Both man and van are in custody. The van had false number plates, but Yard men now know its ownership.

In the early hours of today, William Petersen, manager of the Inferno night club, and Sergius Salsburg, of the club orchestra, were arrested on drug charges. They have made certain statements.

Yard men know of the centre of the operations and expect to make early arrests.

By arrangements with the newspapers the report had been held back until the Final Night Edition.

34

When dark fell, detective officers left the Yard singly, and made their way to West Hendon playing fields. From the top end of the grounds they skirted the swimming pool, crossed the canal fed by the waters of the Welsh Harp, and took up positions giving a view of the Wilson factory premises. Each man had night glasses and walkie-talkie radios. Doctor Manson, Superintendent Jones and Chief Inspector Mackinnon waited in the Doctor's study. Two fast Squad cars with drivers were in readiness in the yard of Central Office.

In his flat in St. Margaret Street, Kenway was aroused by the shrilling of his telephone. 'Reggie . . . Reggie . . . help me,' a voice called in terror. 'Quick . . . no . . . *no.*'

'Margaret!' he shouted back. 'What's the matter . . . Margaret . . . ' The line went dead. It took him a quarter of an hour to reach the Maida Vale flat. The girl's apartment door was open. Inside was disorder. Signs of a struggle were evident in the overturned furniture. He dialled Whitehall 1212 and was switched through to Doctor Manson. 'Doctor,' he said, 'they've taken Margaret. I'm at her place and there's been a hell of a struggle.'

'Come to the factory, Kenway and wait. I think I know where she is, or will be.'

A radio buzzed. 'Calling Central number one,' a voice said. 'Phillips here, sir. A Jaguar has just driven up. A man got out and entered the separate building. It was followed by another car in which were the driver, another man and a woman. She was being helped out.'

'Move!' the Doctor ordered. The waiting cars raced to the Marble Arch corner, turned at speed into and through Edgware Road and continued along Watling Street on to the Welsh Harp. They parked at the end of Ramsay Street, and from there the occupants went on foot to Wilson's factory. Skirting the main building they walked silently in file to the laboratory. Kenway, who had come from the Maida Vale flat moved from his hidden waiting position and joined them.

'How do we get in?' Mackinnon asked in a whisper.

'Follow me,' Manson replied. 'Sergeant Bowles was here earlier and unlocked the storehouse door. The store leads right into the outer laboratory.' A signal called up two of the detective watchers. 'Guard the laboratory front entrance and the factory entrance,' the order came. 'Better have your guns ready.'

One by one Jones, Manson and Mackinnon entered the store and moved stealthily along a passage to the outer laboratory. Voices sounded through the inner door which was slightly ajar. A woman's voice said 'I won't' almost in a whimper.

Manson, automatic in hand, and with Jones alongside him, also armed, threw the door open.

'Stand quite still, gentlemen, please,' he said to the surprised occupants. A startled gasp came from the two men. The laboratory floor held a number of cases packed, and obviously ready for removal. At one end of a bench at the rear of the room, a man was bending over dismantling a piece of apparatus, back towards them.

'Mr. Wilson I presume?' Manson said.

'*Logically accurate as ever, Manson,*' *was the startling reply. Montague Fellowes, Doctor of Science, late of Chairs at Oxford and Harvard, member of the exclusive Dilettantes' Club, stood up straight and turned to face the police officers.*

For the space of a minute — and a minute is a long time — the Doctor stood as though frozen to the spot. He stared at his friend, incredulity on his face, incredulity which turned to anger and then regret.

'You, Fellowes . . . YOU!' His voice was low, so low that it could hardly be heard.

'I, indeed, Manson. But I would rather it had not been you here. You led me up the garden path beautifully with the newspaper report. Timed, of course, to rush me.'

'It *had* to be me, Fellowes. This is murder,' Manson said. He nodded at Jones. Old Fat Man stepped forward and read out three charges of murder.

Kenway entered the room supporting the girl Margaret. 'She had been put in a cupboard,' he said. 'They were going to drop her in the Welsh Harp.'

'They said I had been giving information to Reggie Emerson,' she said.

'I'm not Reggie Emerson, Margaret. I'm . . . ' He appealed to the Doctor. 'This young man, Margaret, is Detective Chief Inspector Kenway, of Scotland Yard and he was on duty in the Inferno Club,' Manson said.

'I don't care who you are,' the girl said. 'I like you and you came in time. Take me home.' Manson nodded permission. (It was two months later, when Kenway had relinquished his bachelor estate, that Margaret learned that the snuff box sniffings, and the hypodermic marks on Kenway's forearms were fakes to induce her to talk!)

★   ★   ★

At ten o'clock the Doctor wandered, grey and tired, into the room of the A.C. He walked slowly, unwillingly. Monty Fellowes had been a particular friend of Sir Edward Allen, in the club and out of it. The A.C. was writing at his desk and looked up. 'Harry,' he said, 'how did it go? Did you get Wilson?'

'There is no Wilson, Edward. The killer of the three people is, however, in the cells.'

'Not Wilson? Well, who is he? You don't look very elated about it.'

'Fellowes.'

The name did not register. 'And the heroin — good work, Harry.'

'*Monty* Fellowes.' Manson stressed the nickname.

'Eh? . . . Monty . . . ' Colour ebbed from the A.C.s face until it was blenched white. He sat bolt, stiffly upright. 'Monty . . . No . . . Oh, my God!' His head sank into his hands. 'Monty . . . why? In heaven's name why?'

'The love of money increases as fast as the money itself increases, Edward. The more a man has, the more he desires to have. Fellowes must have made a large fortune. I thought it was someone else.'

★ ★ ★

The trial lasted only minutes. Fellowes pleaded guilty to a charge of murder, refused legal representation and no evidence was therefore offered.

Epilogue

Sir Edward Allen and Doctor Manson saw him after the trial. 'Sorry about this, Allen,' he apologised.

'But — Barstowe was your friend, your own familiar friend,' the A.C. said.

'Necessity, my dear Allen. Pubilius Syrus wrote as a maxim that a wise man never refuses anything to necessity. Aaronson in that guise talked over a phone unwisely, and was overheard. I had Aaronson followed, and penetrated his disguise, and found out where he changed his disguise twice each night.'

'But the man in Water Street, who was he?'

'I was sorry about that. Barstowe as Aaronson was shadowed there and the word passed to me. I crept up the stairs and killed as I thought Aaronson. I was staggered when Barstowe turned up in the club a couple of nights later. Who was he? I have no idea.'

'The telephone call that kept Barstowe in the club that night — an internal call, of course?' Manson said.

'Of course. To meet secretly at three o'clock the man to whom he had talked unwisely, and who said, via me, that he had vital information. I had an alibi. I had gone to bed and was in my nightclothes, you know.'

They rose to go. The last words were in the language of the Scholars they all three were. Fellowes said, slowly: '*Amici — ad finem. Acherontis pabulum*' (interpreted, it means 'friends — the end. Food for the churchyard). He added: 'Where did I fall down?'

Manson answered in the words of Tacitus, the Roman: '*Acribus initiis, incuriso fine*' and this may be construed as alert in the beginning, negligent in the end. 'I see,' Fellowes said.

He turned to end the scene. At the door of the condemned cell he turned and faced them, smiled, and raised his hand.

'*Vale*,' he said.

It is the ancient word of farewell.

They never saw him again.